WHAT WE ARE BECOMING

WHAT WE ARE BECOMING

2024 Southern Prize & State Fellowships for Literary Arts

HUB CITY PRESS
SPARTANBURG, SC

Book Design Lead: Julie Jarema
Copy Editor: Iza Wojciechowska
Cover Photo: *Abre Camino*, Elliot and Erick Jiménez

SOUTH
ARTS

HUB CITY
PRESS

PUBLISHING
New & Extraordinary
VOICES FROM THE
AMERICAN SOUTH

Spartanburg, SC 29306 | 864.577.9349 | www.hubcity.org

CONTENTS

INTRODUCTION, *John T. Edge* VII

FOREWORD, *Suzette M. Surkamer* XI

RANDI PINK, *Killed the Mockingbird* 3

CAMILLE BOXHILL, *Obeah* 13

CONSTANCE COLLIER-MERCADO, from *None of This Is Real* 25

ASHLEY BLOOMS, from *What the Wolf Wants* 35

MAURICE CARLOS RUFFIN, *Caesara Pittman, or a Negress of God* 57

MELISSA GINSBURG, from *The House Uptown* 63

JOANNA PEARSON, *Amo, Amas, Amat* 85

F.E. CHOE, *The Singing Membrane* 109

YURINA YOSHIKAWA, *Dogwood* 113

CONTRIBUTORS 133

SPONSORS, DONORS, & PARTNERS 137

will pick you up in one place and turn you loose in another. That's the big promise writers make with small fiction: Submit yourself to the world we create, mark changes in the actions or beliefs of my characters, however transformative or slight, and you will depart the story changed, too.

Characters in these brief fictions, excerpted from novels or written as short stories, eat breakfasts of ackee and saltfish and feast on dinners of boiled crawfish. They film wildlife documentaries and blow glass. Scenes take place in a tiny Bronx, New York, apartment and an empty house in rural Dogwood, Tennessee. Beautiful things happen when an artist with dementia leans into her last project. Creepy things happen in an attic stuffed with basinets and a gully strewn with dildos.

Change is a constant in the modern South. Truth is, change has been a constant here across centuries and generations, despite and because of political and social forces that have tried and failed to throttle that dynamism.

These authors embrace that dynamism. Randi Pink of Alabama writes a slant version of *To Kill a Mockingbird*, in which Calpurnia steps beyond the shadow of her character to speak truths. Camille Boxhill of Florida explores family inheritances and magical realism, inspired by Jamaican folklore. Maurice Carlos Ruffin of Louisiana introduces a free woman of color from nineteenth-century New Orleans who takes her revenge with a knife that "shakes like it's singing."

South Arts, founded in 1975 and based in Atlanta, commissioned this collection. Our mission is to advance the vitality of the region through the arts. We make grants and develops initiatives to support organizations and individuals, all to feed an arts ecosystem that tentacles through Alabama, Florida, Georgia, Kentucky, Louisiana, Mississippi, North Carolina, South Carolina, and Tennessee.

The geographies in this collection are messier and truer than that list of states, delineated less by borders and more by migrations. The writers here channel many Souths, defined by porosity and shapeshifting.

Constance Collier-Mercado was born in Chicago, Illinois, and raised in the Bronx, New York. Her family ties reach Mississippi, South Carolina, and Georgia, the state she represents here. Melissa Ginsburg, a native of Houston, Texas, writes about New Orleans, Louisiana, from a base in Oxford, Mississippi. F.E. Choe represents South Carolina. Born in Toronto, Canada, she describes herself as a "Korean American, immigrant daughter, Southern fabulist, and teller of fairy tales."

What We Are Becoming celebrates the inaugural literary cohort of our Southern Prize and State Fellowships. Since 2017, South Arts has recognized visual artists from each of the states in our region. Nine artists annually receive $5,000 State Fellowship awards. Two of those artists receive Southern Prize awards of $25,000 for the winner and $10,000 for the finalist. Now, with this 2024 expansion to include literary arts, those awards and prizes have doubled. For South Arts, this book is a marker of how we will serve literary artists, a glance at what we are becoming.

Historian Lawrence Levine once posited that culture is an ongoing process, never a finite product. And so it is with the South represented in this collection, written by people who live or work or take inspiration from the southern region of the United States. Their South, the place readers get to know here, is forever becoming, in at least two senses of that word.

JOHN T. EDGE
Board Member, South Arts
Author of *House of Smoke*, Fall 2025
Developer Greenfield Farm Writers Residency at the the
University of Mississippi

Dear Readers,

It is my distinct pleasure to welcome you to this inaugural anthology of the Southern Prize and State Fellowships for Literary Arts. The nine authors in this collection are the first recipients of these awards, through which South Arts acknowledges, supports, and celebrates the highest-quality literature being created in the American South.

If you are new to South Arts, or haven't encountered us in a while, allow me to share a brief word about what we do and why. Our mission is advancing Southern vitality through the arts, and we do that by funding, building and amplifying the sector. Why? Because South Arts believes that the arts elevate the region, increasing connectedness and inspiring meaningful change in communities.

Each author in this collection represents a state in our region: Alabama, Florida, Georgia, Kentucky, Louisiana, Mississippi, North Carolina, South Carolina, and Tennessee. Their unique voices and backgrounds begin to sketch a complex, vibrant, and diverse portrait of our region. Our 2024 State Fellows are educators, musicians, historians, advocates, and caregivers. Some are immigrants new to the United States, while others represent families that have been here for generations. Some write with poetic lyricism, while others write with direct, powerful prose. Some are debuting their first novels, while others are established authors with multitudes of well-deserved acclaim. Some write of fantasy, ghosts, and magic, while others write of the realities we all face. Their differences are what compel us to bring their voices together as we explore the complexity of Southern identity.

The nine authors featured in this anthology represent both the culmination of years of planning by South Arts and the beginning of an ongoing journey to further support the writers of our region. The Southern Prize and State Fellowships for Literary Arts is a new annual program in South Arts' portfolio. This first cohort of State Fellows was selected from an application pool of approximately 500 fiction authors who submitted their work for consideration. In the coming years, we will cycle through other genres such as poetry, creative nonfiction, and more as we identify additional authors telling the stories of our region.

This collection is our first step in publishing contemporary Southern literature, and we look forward in the future to highlighting other Southern writers who are telling the story of the South. Thank you to all our donors and partners who helped make this possible, and to you the reader for joining us as we start this celebration with the 2024 Southern Prize and State Fellows.

Sincerely,

SUZETTE M. SURKAMER
President & CEO, South Arts

KILLED THE MOCKINGBIRD

RANDI PINK

The sun had gone blurry, sending every house on the Finches' quaint street into sweaty chaos. Calpurnia, the Finch housekeeper, kneeled in the scarce shade as she scrubbed the dust-prone side porch of her boss, Atticus's, cottage home. Pine and honeysuckle smells fought with freshly cut grass, and by noon, they'd all mixed creating a heady concoction specific to Maycomb. Red remnant from dirt devils dusted nostrils, earlobes, and sometimes, tongues leaving behind the tangy taste of the south.

Calpurnia fanned at large-for-their-size mosquitoes as they floated on the humid air like mean-spirited fairies searching for hosts. Dainty ladies sat cross-legged on the neighboring porches with hand fans and sweet tea, while their dapper husbands hid under the wide brims of stiff fedoras. Those late days of summer were especially long back then, and there would be no relief from the blazing sun until well into the night. The only folks brave enough to take on those Maycomb afternoons were the young'uns and the help, who had no choice in the matter.

Calpurnia had worked for Atticus for many years. And after his wife passed a few years back, she'd stepped in as a mother figure for his children—Jem who was ten now and Jean Louise who was just about six. Calpurnia hummed hymns and kept a watchful eye over them as she cleaned.

Calpurnia grinned at Jean Louise dangling upside down from the tire rope out front, her head brushing so close to the ground that her dark hair picked up tiny particles of red dirt. She shook her head when she saw Jem bite into a not-quite-ready persimmon. Jem's lips went into a disgusted pucker. She'd told him just that morning that there's nothing worse than a tough persimmon, but Jem was getting older, and with age came hardheadedness. Calpurnia cracked the door to yell her I-told-you-so into the humid air, but she heard her name spoken and secretly listened.

"Who is Calpurnia really?" Scout asked, her hair now coated with ruddy dirt.

"Get down from there, Scout, 'fore you fall and break your neck," Jem told her. "And what do you mean who is Calpurnia? She is our maid."

Calpurnia's chest went concave as if she were stuck with a bread knife. *She is our maid,* he'd said, not knowing she was listening. But Calpurnia remembered teaching Jem to write his first letters and then words and then sentences and stories. He was such an eager learner, holding so tight to her copy of *The Velveteen Rabbit* that she'd have to pry it from his palms after he'd fallen asleep. Calpurnia thought of Jean Louise, who was so young when her mother died. She'd promised their dying mother that she'd step forth in her absence and she had done.

Calpurnia loved Jem and Jean Louise deeply and purely. She saw them as mockingbirds left alone in their nest, so she scooped them up and out. Vowing to give of herself, to teach them not

4

only the importance of books and stories and letters and words but morality and fair handedness and God almighty.

Calpurnia swallowed hard and pinched away the tickle forming in the bridge of her nose. Her logical mind told her not to listen further. *It will only hurt*, she knew, but there was no stopping her. After all she'd done for them, she had to know what the Finches truly thought of her.

"Well, I know she is our maid." Jean Louise continued swinging dangerously close to the dirt. "But what is she when she leaves us? What's her story? You never thought to be curious about her, not once?"

Instead of answering, Jem walked briskly to the base of the tire swing and began to shake it violently.

"Jem! Stop it!" Jean Louise hollered out. "Fine, I'll come down. Good Lord, you're trying to kill me to prove a point." She righted herself and leaped safely onto the ground. "I wouldn't have fallen, you know. I never fall."

"Yes," Jem grinned, flashing the mischievous twitch in his left cheek. "I know that."

He then tossed his persimmon as far into the yard as he could throw it and climbed atop the tire swing himself.

"Hey!" Jean Louise folded her arms in tight. "I'm telling Atticus!"

She turned on her bare heels and ran toward the side door. Calpurnia shifted away as not to be caught eavesdropping.

"Wait up," Jem yelled after her. "You can have the swing back, Scout."

"Too late now, I'm telling!" Jean Louise said as she ran head-first into Calpurnia, nearly knocking her sideways.

"Sorry 'bout that, Cal!" Scout yelled but continued running.

On her tail, Jem also collided with Calpurnia followed by the red bucket filled to the brim with dirty water. Thousands of tiny brown bubbles sheeted the wood floors with suds, instantly undoing hours of work.

"That was just an accident, Cal." Jem paused briefly to view the damage. "I am sorry." Jem bowed slightly to show respect and continued chasing his sister.

Calpurnia opened her mouth to scold them, but she didn't want them to hear the shakiness in her voice. She cupped her hands and pulled as many of the bubbles back into the tipped bucket as she could. Her nose began to itch more intensely like it did before a heavy cry. She shook her head, rejecting her useless tears.

Calpurnia lifted herself halfway first and waited as if giving her aching body permission to stand up straight. One leg bent a bit too much and she pressed her palms onto the wet floor for leverage. Her body creaked and cracked as she straightened herself. She was tired, hot, and ready to go home to her husband, Deacon.

When she reached standing position, though her work had been undone at her feet, she thanked the good Lord for to ability to stand.

"Thank you, God," she whispered her gratitude to her Heavenly Father and headed to the hallway shelf for a clean rag.

"Atticus!" Jean Louise yelled from the back of the house. "Atticus!"

"Yes, Scout?" Atticus'ss distinct voice was assertive but also gentle, very southern, and smooth like the magnolia. "I can hear your hollers clear across town at the courthouse."

Atticus was a well-known Maycomb lawyer and had just gotten home from a lengthy day in court. Calpurnia loved to hear Atticus speak and she was not alone. Many in town revered his voice. When he spoke, most folks went into a calm trance of knowing something important awaited their ears. Others, however, jeered him for representing more than just white towns-folk. Calpurnia respected him for it, and though she'd known him for a long time, still enjoyed the powerfulness of his gentle voice.

She pressed herself against the hallway to hide, listen, and forgot the children's assessments of her for a moment. That's when she heard Jem and Jean Louise's dirty bare feet shuffling around Atticus. She imagined the state of the floor. *You'll have to scrub that one too*, she thought and exhaled too loudly.

"Hey, Atticus," Jean Louise started.

"What do you need, Scout?" Atticus replied.

"Jem shook the tire so hard I nearly fell on my..."

"Scout wants to know who Calpurnia is after she's our maid," Jem interrupted, effectively taking attention away from Jean Louise's tattling.

Calpurnia pressed her body even tighter to the wall and held her breath to listen closer and steady her fast-beating heart.

"What could you mean?" Atticus replied in his gentlemanly tenor.

"Jem says she's our maid," Jean Louise replied. "Kind of like she's only that. And I do wonder, Atticus, what else is there?"

Calpurnia leaned forward slightly as not to miss a single word. She heard Atticus squish down into his favorite chair. "Sit, children," he told them. "There's a legal document that should settle this matter once and for all."

There was a short rustling of papers followed by lengthy quiet, but then, he said it.

"Right here in black and white. Notarized by the seal of the great state of Alabama. Calpurnia *is* my maid, you are correct. That is the law of the land, dear children. We will treat her, of course, with the utmost respect and decency. She is a faithful member of this family, that is certain, but simultaneously, the law is the law, understand?"

"Yes, Atticus," Scout and Jem replied in unison.

Calpurnia heard another rustling of papers, and her itchy nose was so bothersome that she could not shake the tears away. She tiptoed down the hall and returned to the suds, allowing her giant tears to disappear into the wetness of the floor. She watched them mix with the dirty water and realization collided with consciousness—BOOM!

She was not here.

She was but a character in a classic.

A ruse.

A wile.

A shadow of a woman.

Jem and Jean Louise were right about her. She was a filler, left to clean the Finch home and take care of the Finch children with no story for herself. Calpurnia wiped her face with her index finger, and her tears were not tears at all. They were permanent ink, for she was only written.

"*To Kill a Mockingbird,*" she said aloud, but did not know why. "Should be a sin To Kill a Mockingbird."

The thousands of bubbles at her feet began to pop one after another until the floor at her feet was clean. She stepped outside and into the afternoon heat but sweat didn't lift from her forehead like it should've. The not-quite-ready persimmons on the tree out front shrank to nothings and the dainty ladies and fedoraed men were nowhere to be seen. Everything vanished until it is only her, standing alone in the tired old town of Maycomb.

As she walked the empty roads, her bare feet kicked up dirt leaving a dusty red ghost to follower her. She leaned forward to pick up one of Ms. Dubose's camellias, likely blown off in the heavy winds from the page before. She then went to smell the flower but there was no aroma. It too had turned to ink in her hands.

Calpurnia toured the Finches' quiet area, gathering as many plants and flowers as she could hold in her palms—Mayella Ewell's blood red geraniums, Maudie Atkinson's floppy azaleas, she even found a clump of scuppernongs hanging wild on a white fence.

On her way back to the Finches' porch, Calpurnia saw a feather peeking from a knothole in the Radleys' highest oak tree. Although no one was about, Calpurnia approached the Radley yard with caution. She looked left and then right and tipped closer to the hole in the mighty oak. After one last glance around, she reached in to retrieve a feathered quill and a scroll of frayed paper. Eager to leave Radley ground, Calpurnia returned to the Finches' porch and made a pile with her findings.

The flowers and scuppernongs quickly liquefied into a small pool of ink swirled with the light pink of the azalea, the bright red of the geranium, and green tinges from the scuppernongs. From her pocket, she lifted the old-fashioned quill and scroll—a gift from the Radleys' tree.

Calpurnia looked from the quill to the scroll at least three times. She felt her forehead scrunch into confusion. None of this made sense at all. What was this? How was this happening? She couldn't shake the thought that she was simply written, like an unsupported supporting character in a book. Could she be dreaming this entire thing up?

She pinched her forearm, hard. "Ouch!"

Rubbing at her aching arm, Calpurnia fixed her thoughts on idyllic Maycomb. The flowers were in full bloom spanning all colors of the rainbow. The leaves on the trees danced like they were caught in mad green fits. Children swung as high as their little legs could take them and then they'd leap leaving lines in the soft green grass or goopy red dirt to see who'd leaped the farthest. Even in the height of the heat, that side of Maycomb was a pleasure to reside in.

But alas, she could not. Fore she was born Black. And as she'd just overheard spoken by her beloved Jean Louise, Mister Jem, and Atticus, in this book, she was only the maid.

"I am more," she whispered aloud to no one. "I am a wife. A mother in my own right. A reader. A teacher. If I had my way, I'd be a librarian or a book shop owner, reading the hours away in quiet. My favorite book is *Sense and Sensibility*. My favorite character within that book is Marianne Dashwood who skips through her own pages like a sprite with her fancy words and demeanors, but she is the same as me."

Calpurnia's voice began to rise like a slow thunderstorm as she paced the front yard of the Finch home. "Yes, I am a Black woman in the south of Alabama, but we are more similar than different— Marianne and I. Allow me to quote this masterpiece and show myself there! *Marianne Dashwood was born to an extraordinary fate. She was born to discover the falsehood of her own opinions, and to counteract, by her conduct, her most favourite maxims.*"

"Of course, I've memorized the texts!" Calpurnia said, now breathless. "I've scoured *Sense and Sensibility* for a passage assigning value to a woman and this is what I find every time. Me!" She yelled out, her voice echoing the old-world street. "Burying my passions because they mean not one thing to the wide world outside of the confines of fiction. I've searched my small world for answers, and I find myself. Brilliant. Kind. Considerate. Underestimated. Minimized and buried under the heavy weight of maid to the great Atticus Finch."

Calpurnia quieted, lowering her voice to a whisper. "I've found multitudes in books. Each page is a new life lived through hundreds of thousands of sets of eyes. What I would not give for the opportunity to write my own story. My own family..."

She closed her eyes and breathed out any thought of the Finches to make space for her own unwritten loved ones.

"Deacon." She smiled into the empty air. "My love."

She saw his strong, broad shoulders in her mind's eye. Powerful enough to lift her easily with one arm and continue reading his book with the other. His love for the written word exceeded his strength, and that's why she'd married him. Calpurnia could watch him read over his glasses for hours. In that peculiar moment on the Finch porch, she longed for him.

"See," she spoke lowly to empty Maycomb. "I am a wife."

She searched her mind and heart for more tender spots.

"Eli," Calpurnia said with her eyes still closed. "Agnes."

Eli and Agnes, her precious grandbabies, were teenagers already and she could hardly believe it. It felt like just yesterday she'd taught them to read, and formed their Inkwell Book Club, but it'd been years.

"See that? I've lived many lives outside of my vocation."

Behind her closed eyes, Calpurnia saw the four of them—Deacon, Agnes, Eli, and herself—sitting around their tiny oak dining table discussing their Inkwell books. She heard herself laugh at their bickering over which book would be chosen next.

Eli would push for Langston Hughes as usual, while Agnes would nearly come to blows for *Mrs. Dalloway*'s sake. Deacon accepted any selection without protest since he'd read anything at all with joy. That tiny oak table was where Calpurnia came alive.

"I should've been more than the maid in a novel," Calpurnia sat on the Finch front stoop and said sternly. "I have cultivated love of books and family, and I am more."

Who is Calpurnia anyway?

Law is law.

Notarized by the great state of Alabama.

Calpurnia is my maid.

The joy she felt thinking of her loved ones was interrupted and the tears were so intense that they burned at her sinuses. She lifted the scroll and feathery quill and began to write feverishly. She was not thinking as she wrote. Her heart took over the quill, spilling its pain into words. Calpurnia let the scroll float down right and left and right and left until it landed on the spotless porch, she'd cleaned hundreds of times before.

And there it was.

On the fictional porch of the fictional hero's quaint home from the fictional story that had taken the world by storm for generations. A new beginning. Written by an unexplored character who always deserved more.

I am more than just their maid. I'd assumed everyone knew that. Every one of you who read that book or watched that movie. I was the concrete underneath your novel. I was the load-bearing walls, silently holding this house up. Shhh, listen. That's the sound of you assuming I'm angry about it. I am not angry or weary or dwelling, why? You've already killed this mockingbird. Now, I'm Betula nigra shedding myself smooth. Yellow in the autumn. Flowering in the spring but... Spring is over for me. I'm now standing still in full sun or part shade or dry or wet Alabama red dirt or whatever you decide to give me that morning. No maintenance, no problem. Plant me where you need me and expect a quiet harvest but do not be surprised when you find out... You killed this here mockingbird already. I died quiet so Jem and Jean Louise and Atticus could emerge from my soil and grow on. But this time, dear God, and reader, I hold the quill and you're reading this, so you likely read that novel or saw that movie.

Welcome to my side of the story.

With love and a bit of anger,

Calpurnia

OBEAH

CAMILLE BOXHILL

Prologue

Growing up, I heard all sorts of stories. In Mandeville, a young woman walks home from work and feels she is being followed. She looks over her shoulder. No one is there. When she looks ahead again, she sees her dead father standing in front of her. Just as quickly as he appears, he is gone. The following morning, the young woman's mother says that her late husband appeared in her dreams, telling her to warn their daughter of walking alone at night.

In St. Mary, a little girl falls gravely ill. The child's mother tries every herb and bush she can find. Nothing works. A friend tells her that a neighbor is to blame for the child's sudden illness. The mother digs the ground beneath the daughter's window, where she finds a glass bottle of colored liquid. In it are strands of floating hair. She destroys the jar, and her daughter makes a full recovery.

In Kingston, a woman suspects a friend is stealing from her home. She purchases new earrings. Weeks later, they are gone. She is gifted a decadent body butter. Within days, the cream is gone, her knuckles left to ash over in dehydration. Finally, she buys a pair of shoes and fixes them to swell the feet of any thief who wears them. The following week, she receives a call from her friend. She says her foot is swollen like a jackfruit, and she cannot walk.

Others call it voodoo, witchcraft even. But we call it obeah. It's the dark underbelly of the paradise island. Outlawed in many Caribbean nations, its practitioners are forced to work in secrecy.

After a long day of stifling heat, bottomless cups of rum cream, and barely audible melodies humming from ancient wood-paneled speakers, my family gathers in the kitchen exchanging embarrassing tales from their childhood that seem to grow more exaggerated with each retelling.

I watch from the front room for a moment before slipping onto the veranda, carefully closing the iron gate behind me.

Outside, it's dusk. I imagine the sun and horizon kissing in the distance, the waning moon looking on from above. It will be dark by the time I arrive. It's better that way. Fewer people on the road meant fewer conversations with potential questions that would be met with untruthful responses.

Darkness cloaks the parish, snuffing out the once fire-golden skies. I try to quell a pang of guilt as I think about Mama, wondering what she would say if she knew my plans. Would she blame herself? Disown me?

I near my final destination, and my eyes search the darkness for the marker: raised flags on bamboo posts.

The gate is all that separates us now. It's where I pause, indulging my second thoughts, and consider the lengthy list of options I've already exhausted. I can still go home. Forget tonight happened, that I ever dared to play this game. Go back to—

A low creak disrupts the night's silence, the front door opening slightly in the distance. She is expecting me.

Mama says anything done in the dark must come to light, but I know how to keep a secret.

Chapter One

Candace took a deep breath before retrieving the key from the inner pocket of her purse, readying herself. She unlocked the deadbolt and heard the latch click open. Pushing gently on the door, she entered.

"Hey, Mama," Candace said.

"Candace? Quick, come and turn this breadfruit, please," her mother yelled from the kitchen. Candace could smell the ackee and saltfish in the air. Her mother always made a fuss over meals whenever she visited. Sundays were their standing "mommy-and-me" time. It had become a tradition over the years. But her mother was thrilled to hear that she planned to spend the night that Saturday.

Candace removed her shoes and hung her jacket in the front closet. The house had changed substantially over the years, undergoing staggered renovations until nothing was left of the past except familiar smells and sounds.

As she walked towards the kitchen in the back of the house, she glimpsed herself in her mother's antique floor mirror; it was one of the few items from the original house and their only family heirloom. Despite the interior designer's cajoling, her mother had refused to part with it or compromise on the recommended "strategic placement" in one of the lesser-used bedrooms. Candace met her eyes in the mirror's reflection. In an instant, she was five years old with plaited pigtails, eyes too big for her face, and buck teeth that would later require three years of braces to correct. She was back in their old living room. Her father sat in his favorite leather armchair. It was a hideous thing that had worn so much over the years that the leather had started to crack, pulling away from the cushion. Sometimes, when he got up from the chair, there were sprinkles of black leather fragments stuck to the back of his head. She and her mother would laugh to themselves.

The summer her father left was unbearably hot, the days insufferably long. The air was warm and thick like mannish water, and Candace remembered how the heat had made her stockings stick to the back of her legs on those Saturday morning walks to church. Once their trio became a duo, her mother, an already religious woman, had turned even further toward her faith, leaning on an unseen God with the crushing weight of her grief.

Candace felt the stares and heard the murmurs of neighbors. Pairs of judgmental eyes pelted her back. Hushed voices from fake friends donning painfully wide smiles with too many teeth—crooked, yellowed, occasionally false.

As a child, Candace—like most children—took things quite literally. So, when she had overheard church sisters tell her mother that the Lord heals the brokenhearted and binds their wounds, Candace decided that she would aid the healing process. One afternoon, following church, she'd busied herself by the stove like she had seen her mother do countless times before, boiling a pot of water and infusing it with cerasee. She boiled the bitter leaves and strained them in case heartbreak came with belly aches. She squeezed the juice of a lime and mixed it with honey in case heartbreak came with a cough. She placed both cups on her mother's bedroom nightstand. Then, she crept to the bathroom and emptied the contents of her mother's medicine cabinet—the one with the band-aids and bandages, rubbing alcohol and peroxide, and all the things her mother turned to when Candace was sickly. The syrups and chewable tablets her mom administered when the fragrant herbal infusions didn't do the trick were kept in the drawer just below the sink. Candace pulled the drawer and it jammed, its contents clanging against each other. It was secured with one of those impossible child locks. She was hugging her self-made medic kit, gathering the pile in her arms, when the bathroom door swung open. Startled, Candace dropped the tub of Vicks VapoRub she'd had sandwiched between her elbow and side. It rolled until it met her mother's foot, where she stood in the doorway.

"I...I...just wanted to help." Candace stuttered her way through an explanation that had made more sense in her head than it did vocalized—detailing her mother's personalized care plan.

It was quiet for a beat before her mother's explosive laughter broke the silence. Tears sprung to her eyes, and she doubled over with laughter, using a hand to brace herself against the bathroom's doorframe. And, for the first time since her father left, Candace had believed everything would be alright.

And as quickly as the memory had come, it was gone, losing shape like falling sand. She tried to hold on to it, but the fine grains seeped between her fingers until there was nothing left.

When Candace entered the kitchen, her mother was standing at the sink, wearing a waffle-knit lounge set. She was a small woman, her mother, standing barely over five feet. What she lacked in height, she more than made up for in curves: generous bust, naturally cinched waist, full hips and butt to match. Her skin was the color of toffee that darkened to a deep mocha during the summer months. Her petite stature was smoke and mirrors because absolutely nothing else about the woman was small. Her presence was significant, commandeering space in every room she entered. Her voice, so boisterous, carried farther than any voice should.

Candace kissed her mother on the cheek before turning her attention to the breadfruit on the cooktop. She flipped a crescent-moon-shaped wedge of breadfruit, revealing the golden-brown side with its darkened edges.

Her mother stood next to her, adding more scotch bonnet peppers to the pot of ackee. They moved effortlessly in the space together, going from the stove to the sink and back to the stove. The original kitchen, with its outdated cabinetry and permanently stained laminate, had a tight galley layout that didn't lend itself to multiple occupants. Growing up, Candace had loved to sneak snacks while her mother prepared dinner. Thrust into a poorly choreographed waltz, the two would twirl and try desperately to avoid stepping on each other's toes. Candace missed those moments. Things were simpler then.

"Shame yuh did miss church today," her mother said, not trying to mask her judgment.

There it was. Candace knew it wouldn't be long before her mother would mention church.

"Sorry, Mama. I had to catch up on some work this morning."

Her mother mumbled something to herself. Soon, she'd move on to the next topic, the latest story or family drama. Last week's hot topic was her neighbor Peta-Gaye's surprise marriage.

"You memba Peta-Gaye?" her mother asked.

"I don't." Candace did.

"Sherry's daughter. She did go uh foreign fi school."

"Oh, yes," Candace said. Her mother planned to tell the story regardless; whether Candace remembered Peta-Gaye was of minimal importance.

"Sherry did haffi walk an' beg. Peta-Gaye go take up man with plenty money an' a send two shillings give her madda now."

Candace rolled her eyes. Her back was to her mother, so it was safe. The truth was that Candace already knew about Peta-Gaye: the man, the marriage, the new job. If the grass was greener on the other side, her lawn was perfectly manicured and lushly land-scaped with heavenly high hornbeam hedges to keep the rest of the world out.

Her mother had eventually moved on to discuss other things,

but Candace's mind lingered on Peta-Gaye's picture-perfect life, wondering, "What if?"

Candace's mother was a hopeless romantic who anxiously awaited the day her daughter's ring finger—heavy with promise—would declare her newly minted status as fiancée and soon-to-be wife. Sometimes, Candace imagined her mother ticking off the passing days of her singledom like convicts tallying their time of imprisonment.

When dinner was done, Candace plated their food and placed it at the kitchen's island, where they usually ate.

"Say grace." It wasn't a question. Never mind that Candace had her own issues with her faith and wasn't a practicing Christian, the same set of rules had always applied in her mother's home. Candace's mother was a God-fearing woman and subscribed wholeheartedly to the word of Christ, denouncing anything that couldn't be supported by the Bible. Raised Seventh-day Adventist, she still spent the entirety of her Saturdays at church. Candace remembered early morning Bible study as a child. She had especially loved the coin purse that held her modest offering because it was made in the likeness of her mother's designer handbag. As she got older though, church on Saturdays became an unavoidable inconvenience. One that kept her from friends' birthday parties and sporting events and Saturday morning cartoons.

"God is great. God is good. Let us thank Him for our food. By His blessings, we are fed. Give us, Lord, our daily bread. Amen."

"Amen."

A few moments later, Candace's mother looked at her phone and sucked her teeth. Despite not being particularly tech-savvy, she spent a shocking amount of time bouncing between Facebook and WhatsApp on her smartphone. Candace's cousins must have posted photos of their children dressed for their annual All Hallows' Eve celebration. Halloween was her mother's favorite holiday to hate.

"Coo yah, pickney uh dress like devil," her mother said as she scowled at her phone's screen. "Man nuh fi trouble God and pickney nuh fi worship di devil."

"Ma," Candace said, hoping to distract her. "Let's just eat."

It was just after ten that night when her mother retired to bed. Still in her day's clothes, which she'd been wearing since dawn, Candace stepped into her bedroom. With its original parquet floors and dusty blush wallpaper, it was like entering a time capsule, the only room that had remained unchanged since the renovation, original trim and window casing intact.

A piece of her childhood—her teenage years—frozen in time. When she inhaled deeply, she swore the room smelled the same: Tide laundry detergent; the warm, boozy smell of artificial vanilla from the wall plug-in; and the slightest notes of talcum powder that her mother sprinkled between the bed's flat and fitted sheets. The medley of scents would linger on her clothes, revealing itself to her again only once she had left.

She ran her fingers along the foot of the sleigh bed, following the direction of the wood grain. The wall next to her bed was a carefully curated collage, a mashup of items: posters of Beyoncé and Adele, a *Do the Right Thing* art print, *Teen Vogue* cutouts, and a University of Virginia felt pennant flag, her last addition before leaving for college.

She removed her jacket and went to place it in the closet. When she slid the hanging garment bags—filled with her mother's out-of-season clothing—the opening revealed her old dollhouse. She shuffled the nearly three-foot dollhouse from its hiding place. She kneeled on the floor in front of it, feet tucked beneath her. Inside the two-story Victorian replica home was a family of two. Mother and daughter lay lifeless on the floor of the parlor. Candace picked up the mother. Her body felt disfigured under her clothes. She lifted the dress's hem, and two flattened cotton balls fell to the floor. The memory rushed back to her. Growing up, she had desperately wanted a sibling and pestered her mother ceaselessly about a new addition. A quick call to the stork, she had thought, and it would all be sorted. She had known nothing about babies' origin stories. Soon after, she would stop playing with the dollhouse, moving on to more sophisticated toys. The home was packed away: the only child and her mother, pregnant in perpetuity. Candace placed everything back as it was inside the closet.

Later that night, unable to sleep, Candace ventured downstairs. She had to pass her mother's bedroom on the second floor. The old house once wove a tapestry of noise—the hiss of a radiator, the squeak of a dusty door hinge, the hum of the old fridge— that all seemed especially loud in the still of the night. These sounds—the skeleton of the house—came creaking to life only to dissolve into quiet nothingness by morning. Since the renovation, the floors of the home no longer creaked. It had been scrubbed of all the little quirks Candace had grown to love in childhood.

She reached the landing outside her mother's room and, not hearing a sound, carefully pushed open the door to her bedroom.

When Candace was little, her mother would often visit her at night. Her unexpected drop-ins interrupted Candace's late-night readings. She'd be under her covers, working a case alongside Nancy Drew, the book's small print illuminated by the dim glow of a clip-on reading light, when, suddenly, she'd hear her mother's footsteps approaching. Quickly, she'd fake a deep sleep, carefully controlling her breathing. Inhale. One Mississippi. Two Mississippi. Exhale. One Mississippi. Two Mississippi.

Now, she watched as her mother slept, her chest rising and falling peacefully. She stood there for a moment before closing the door, the latch clicking quietly into place.

She went downstairs to the living room and scanned the

built-ins that bookended the fireplace. Camouflaged among her mother's Encyclopedia Britannica set from the '90s—another relic of the past that she had refused to part with—was a leather photo album that contained a detailed catalogue of her mother's early years in America and Candace's first few years of life. It had been her favorite picture book, and, in many ways, it still was—the excessive handling evidenced by the album's loosened binding.

There was Candace at her first birthday party, hair in two puffs, drowning in a sea of ruffles. Her cheeks covered in white frosting, a chunk of cake in her tiny fist. Her mother stood behind her in a matching linen set and a fluffy, pin-curled bob that stopped just shy of her shoulders. Her head thrown back in laughter. Beside it, Candace, the lion in her grade school's recreation of *The Wizard of Oz*, captured mid-roar in front of the auditorium's stage. She'd auditioned for the part of Dorothy, only to be cast as her hairy and cowardly companion. While she may not have been the lead, she was inarguably the best dressed. Her mother and grandmother had made sure of that, spending weeks on sketches, sourcing fabrics, and finally sewing it all together. It was something of a school legend, this costume, and one of the most talked-about pieces for years to come. A fur jacket with matching fur collar. A bodysuit with brown, feathered hems. Wheat-colored Timberland boots on her feet. Her hair, picked into an afro, framed an immaculately painted lion face. On the next page, there was her mother, holding a doe-eyed Candace and pointing to the camera. Who, Candace wondered, was behind the lens?

As a child, Candace had spent hours studying the photo album, scouring it for details about her father—a shadow lurking in a corner, a blurred reflection in a mirrored surface, anything that would indicate his presence. There wasn't a single photo, an item of clothing, or a piece of jewelry that could corroborate his existence. Instead, he existed solely in her mind—fragments of a man gathered from disparate sources and constructed into a sort of Frankenstein-type creation. She felt it shameful, at times, the tug of longing and curiosity she had for a man who had abandoned them all those years ago and made no effort to reconnect since.

Perhaps the thing that puzzled Candace the most was that, although he had left her without support—financial or otherwise—her mother never spoke ill of her father. She simply didn't speak of him at all. In fact, hardly anyone did. On the odd occasion, her aunt might let slip her disdain for him, but that was it.

The pages of the photo album were thick, reinforced with cardboard backing and a protective film over each adhesive page. Candace went to turn a page when she noticed that it felt particularly thick. She brought the album close to her eyes and realized two pages were stuck together, something she had never noticed before. She used her fingernail to loosen the edges of the pages and carefully pried them apart.

Too shocked to move, Candace stared fixedly at the photo on the page. She recognized the living room in the photo as theirs, pre-renovation. It was Christmas. An artificial pine tree aggressively decorated in silver and gold tinsel stood in the corner. There was her mother, younger, her laugh lines not quite as deep, her jawline still sharp with youthfully taut skin. And there he was: a man behind her. He was of a darker complexion and tall, though her mother's poofed hair concealed his face. He was placing something around her neck, a herringbone chain that matched his own, tucked but just visible, under the collar of his polo shirt.

How could I have missed this, she thought. *I must have flipped through this album hundreds of times.*

She outlined the figures of her mother and this mystery man with her finger, taking in her discovery. Her mind—overstimulated with the night's findings and unsure of how to act on them—drifted to all sorts of scenarios. Familiar ones she had perfected during childhood. Now, newer ones with this faceless man recast as her father.

That night, Candace was walking through the home, only the rooms were all empty. The furniture was gone, and the walls were bare. She opened a door to the upstairs hallway and saw a man standing with his back to her. She called to him, but he didn't respond. She yelled louder, and he began walking away from her. She ran after him, but the distance between them only grew. She was crying, then. Why won't he stop? Why won't he look at her? Where has he gone?

"Candace," her mother said loudly.

Candace started from her sleep, her eyes adjusting to the harsh morning light that shot like lasers through the cracks in the wooden shudders.

"Why are you sleeping down here?" her mother asked.

"Oh," she said groggily as she sat upright on the couch. "I was having some trouble sleeping, so I came downstairs to watch TV."

"Mmm," her mother considered this. She looked from Candace to the blank television screen. "You should have woken me."

"It was late. I didn't want to disturb you." Candace noticed that the photo album was now closed and sitting on the edge of the side table next to the couch.

"Right," her mother paused, still looking at Candace as if searching for something on her face. "Well, come," she said, tapping her leg. "Brush your teeth and wash your face. Help me start breakfast."

When her mother was gone and just out of earshot—pans clanking in the kitchen—Candace reached out for the photo album. She quickly flipped through and—to her horror—made it to the end: no stuck pages, no new photos, no mystery man.

Doubt had quickly infiltrated her mind, and with it the fear that perhaps she had imagined it all.

In her mind's eye, she could still see her mother—in her twenties, sparkling, smiling back at her from the image. The photo was real. She was sure of it.

from NONE OF THIS IS REAL

CONSTANCE COLLIER-MERCADO

December made its way to the Bronx each year, gift wrapped in a perfectly grimy, flea market tattered, X-mas snow globe, likely hand-me-down knocked off from among the finest of Southern Boulevard's wares. Which is to say that it was nothing like the ornamental snow globes Traci Stewart had bought for her twin daughters so long ago. For starters, December in the Bronx was not a thing to be either bought or sold, held, or confined. It was a single throbbing spacetime coordinate born of nobles and thieves. Since Traci's girls were born of a just right dress and one fine young husband she wasn't much interested in authenticity. It was an aesthetic she was after. Especially since her husband had so quickly gone the way of youth.

When they'd dated in college, L. had been the perfect boyfriend. And later, after graduation, he'd been a better than average husband—considerate, dependable, good in bed. Traci figured that last part at least should count for something since she was never really cut out to be anyone's wife. Still one day something like a bridge just sprung up between them. Or maybe it was a highway. Certainly not anything meant to bring the pair together but instead some hulking piece of architecture that could only signal departure.

It would be easier if she could name that highway *Mistress* or *Workaholic* or, worst of all, *Deadbeat*. But L. was too much of a straight-and-narrow guy to offer that final satisfaction. In the end, she had emotionally checked out, long before he finally agreed to sign the divorce papers. It was even longer still before he boarded his midnight train out of the city, done with hoping that if he stuck around, she might work her way back to him. No one had the heart to tell Gladys she'd got it all wrong.

The real tragedy to their ending was twofold: Mali and Mecca would now be another broken home statistic in the eyes of those who made sure such things mattered. And if Traci foolishly thought life as a single parent couldn't be that hard, circumstances quickly wiped the rosy tint from her glasses. New York in the nineties was full of just as much hope and promise as her young marriage had been in the eighties. There was a Black mayor, she was a college educated professional, and living in the poorest borough of the city came with the silver lining that there was nowhere to go but up. Traci was convinced that historic Longwood and nearby Hunts Point were the place to be when a wave of industrial apartments and retail storefronts inevitably rolled through. So she bought a rundown three-story walkup on unassuming Beck Street and waited for an urban housing boom that never came.

In the wake of this ultimate betrayal, Traci craved the superficial comfort of those glittery baubles, meant to dangle from matching gold necklaces, almost as much for herself as she craved it for her girls. Snow globe pendants were a silly thing to obsess over, she knew, but of all the preoccupations that kept her up at night, saving for those necklaces was the only one that delivered any joy to her doorstep. It wasn't that her life was so terrible with two young girls, surrounded by the same old neighbors, but she hated the thought that she too might be just another of the same old neighbors. Over the years, the mayor eventually changed but not much else. Wasn't the expressway that blew through their lives supposed to bring some kind of progress with it? Wasn't that the thing she'd fought so hard for, to the point that she'd fought her damned husband away too? But year after year sped by and in her rear view was always the same paper-pushing job with plenty responsibility but no raise, the same garbage infested streets with no resources, and the same pile of bills that kept multiplying like a cancer. She quickly learned that worse than living in a borough with nowhere to go but up was living in the borough that had stagnated while everyone else moved on.

If life was determined to remind her of her lower-rung place in the world, Traci wanted her daughters to have something that would remind them to keep looking up. The miniature city inside their snow globes would never change either, forever vibrant and glittering with promise. Something about that felt right. So she saved her coins and on the occasion of the twin's 10th birthday she gifted them each the tiny time capsule she wanted more than anything for her own life. She longed for it with such fervor there should have been no surprise when at least one of her children rebelled and dared fall in love with the Bronx as it really was—raw, unpolished, and pungent with the stench of survival. That child was her now seventeen-year-old, Mecca, who on this particular afternoon had just finished a mandatory session of winter math tutoring and was off with friends exploring the familiar catacombs of their borough.

A trinket which shaped the boundaries for much of Mecca's world view, she loved the Bronx fiercely. If you traded the typical snow globe waterfall of snowflakes for boot-print-blackened glaciers, swapped the gingerbread house at center for an eighteen-story asthma attack, and replaced its wind-up cracker jack music with a blend of *Double R What* and *Guasa, Guasa*, one could almost picture the surroundings as she and her friends stalked day into night, marking invisible borders around their neighborhood fortress.

A filmy grey smear of exhaust clung to the air all around and Mecca liked the casual challenge of projecting herself and the dreams of her neighbors into vibrant bright color outside that fog. This wasn't a matter of casting them outside their circumstances so much as giving the block a Technicolor makeover from the likes of her G-ma's switch-dial black-and-white TV into HD realness. She was so enthralled with this laying claim to herself, or at least to her block, that she didn't at first notice they'd actually left her neighborhood several avenues ago. When the wide expanse of sky above gave way to steel pillars and double beams, signaling they'd crossed under the elevated number two train, she finally took stock.

"I thought we were going to the park by your house?" Mecca slowed her stride as she realized her friends had veered off course from their favorite haunt.

"We are. I just gotta make a stop first." Brianna held her breath, hoping Mecca wouldn't ask anything else.

"A stop where? In the opposite direction? Cause the Point is back that way."

Traci needed to get up. This old sofa was no better for her back than the cramped office chair and computer screen she'd sat in front of all day. She stretched her arms above her head and bowed her tired limbs toward the ceiling. She was irritable and didn't know if it was Todd in Accounting or the cold weather or her motherly instincts, but she wanted a cigarette. Through the open window she could hear people outside arguing on the street. Someone wanted payment and wasn't leaving without it.

Someone else thought that bitch was crazy to be demanding so much when he knew her situation. Several others just wanted them both to shut the fuck up. Traci could sympathize with each. Wanting anything too badly always led to heartache. Like how it was 6:45 and something in the fading sunlight had already tipped her off that Mecca would be late.

The floorboards creaked as she stood and trudged her way downstairs to the kitchen. Everyone said she should get with the times but they didn't understand that old habits never really die, they just migrate. There was still nothing like the feel of a warm stove pressed against her hip while a different kind of heat dangled between her fingers. If she couldn't have the quick hit of tobacco she craved, only one other thing would satisfy. He answered on the third ring and she released the tangle of telephone wire from its growing vice around her pointer.

"Your daughter is working my last nerve, L."

Lindsey didn't bother asking, 'Who is this?' He just gave a short laugh. "Your daughter says the same thing about me."

"Because it's true." She smiled. "How is Mali? David doesn't have her running the street too bad, does he?"

"They're meeting up later. She got sick of me trying to old-man bond with her and decided to go rob a bank." Lindsey weighed his next words carefully, testing out the taste of them on his tongue before release. "Nephew said to tell his favorite Auntie 'Hi' by the way."

"Tell him I said 'Hey, baby! But you really can stop calling me that now.'"

"That last part for him or me?"

"Both. You could have let it ride though." Traci shuffled over to the kitchen counter and perched herself atop the wooden butcher block. Her mood, like her feet, floated up from its place along the dull linoleum.

"I could, but where's the fun in that?" he quipped.

"With your girlfriend. What's her name again? Sonia?"

Lindsey laughed out loud. Long boisterous cries echoed through the receiver. Traci leaned back against the cabinet and waited for him to finish.

Between heaving gasps, he sputtered, "She said to tell you 'Hello' too. You're her…" He was practically crying with each word. "You're her favorite jealous ex-wife!"

"If she were smart, she'd keep you better occupied," Traci countered, but Lindsey was still laughing. She pretended not to notice.

"You're the one who called," he reminded; then, sensing the tone of her silence, he let the teasing drop. "What's up?"

"I just told you. Or weren't you listening?"

"I heard. There's something else, though. You sound like you need a light. You didn't quit again, did you?" Traci ignored this questioning too.

"You don't know how your daughter tries me. She's late for curfew. Again."

"It's not even dark yet." If Lindsey was settling down for the night, he didn't let on. The incredulity in his voice was palpable. She was glad he couldn't see her pronounced eye roll.

"Don't worry. It will be in a few minutes."

"Traci, be reasonable…"

"She might not graduate, L. That's unreasonable."

Traci flexed one leg toward the refrigerator door and pulled it open with the tip of her toe. It irked her that he could play act this young, hip dad for the girls' benefit but had refused to be anything more than stodgy husband when she'd needed it. Even now, she could hear the mollifying drone he reserved exclusively for their conversations.

"I know," he was saying. "And I've talked to her about the grades. I'll talk to her again."

"What is there to discuss? It's not like she can't pass. She's doing this to spite me."

"Can you just trust me to get through to her without dropping a hammer?" She wanted to drop something on his head for the way he staunchly refused to take her side.

"That's the problem, L. You're a feather." Still, she wished he could be some easily accessible comfort on the shelf of her life. As things stood, she couldn't even find the Tabasco fried eggs from this morning's breakfast.

"No, I'm her father. And it's Lindsey, not L."

Traci let out a deep sigh, "Okay, L. You're the vision of fatherly discipline. A regular charging bull. Fine. But can we not pretend that talking is going to fix this?"

"It could if you were willing to listen. But you won't even get my name right. My mother named me one whole Lindsey Stewart. You married and divorced a Lindsey. Not some letter of the alphabet."

"Oh, don't bring Ms. Pauline into this." Traci spotted a jar of pickles crowded onto the bottom rung and reached for a hot and spicy. "I talk to your momma more than you do. She says you need to change your draws and come see her on the other side of town." The briny spear waved in her face like her usual hand-rolled. "And me calling you L. is just an old love tap. We have history. Why this dog and pony like I don't know your name?"

"Look, me and my smelly draws aren't itching for a fight but there is this thing that you do—"

"What thing?"

"This thing where you unsee a person. Disappear all the inconvenient parts you don't like. You never were a fan of my country name so much as the look of me you thought might someday fit a better role."

"Well, I feel pretty damn tethered to your current role." Traci could tell the moment the chili and vinegar mix hit her stomach. It was a welcome distraction from the annoyance also brewing there. "Every time I try missing us, back in the day on the phone til midnight—no stove, all heat—running up someone else's bill, you go and drag me back to our same tired ending. You're this landline choking the joy out of everything."

"And some days you hate me for it. Thanks for proving my point."

"Fuck you. If we're talking about disappearing people, aren't you tired of begging me to be somebody's Auntie again? I don't guilt you over that little pastime. I laugh and let it roll off. But let me even think of what comes after K and here you are reminding me how Pauline Stewart named you. Well, my name isn't Auntie or Pauline. How about that?"

Lindsey didn't argue the point. "I thought you and her still got along?"

"We do. She doesn't ask me to be something I'm not. Your mother's better than either of us at knowing how to love a person."

"Why didn't you call her?"

"I should have." There was a beat of silence over the line that felt heavier than before. Traci cut it off before the feeling could take root. "Are we talking about Mecca or why you and I broke up? Because I'm bored, L. So very bored reliving that failure."

"Me too. It repeats, though, whether we like it or not. I'm just trying to stop it rippling over the girls."

"Please tell me what is so wrong with wanting good things for my children? You act like me pushing Mecca toward her potential is the same as not seeing her."

"Her in the future, maybe. Do you see who she is right now?"

"A spoiled teenager throwing a tantrum."

"Tell me some more how reasonable you're being."

"Listen, I give these girls everything. Mecca could be in private school right now, actually being challenged, but she threw that back in my face like she does everything else. How am I the bad guy?"

"So she's spoiled because you give her everything. But she's throwing a tantrum for not wanting it handed to her. Do I have that right?"

"No, you've got it wrong. You're not here, L. You pop in for a quick visit and think you understand but raising two children in this city doesn't come with easy answers."

"You didn't have to be alone in this."

"Sure I did. No one told you to pick up and leave just because I didn't want 'Us.' You did that all on your own and you did it to punish me. Otherwise, why not stay and make peace with being unwanted but maybe also a better father?"

He was saying something about her being "unfair" and "misrepresenting how it all ended" when a loud banging from downstairs made Traci drop the pickle jar.

"Damnit!" She wiggled across the counter to avoid broken glass and reached for a broom.

"What's going on?"

"Just somebody playing games at my front door. Their little hood soap opera was cute at first but if I cut my foot they gone piss me off."

"Are you sure everything's okay? No one trying to break in?" The concern in his voice was endearing after the tension of the last few minutes.

"Why? You catching the next flight over?"

"Be serious, please," Lindsey scolded. But Traci figured they were overdue for a change of subject.

"I am being serious. Would Sonia not approve?"

"You sure know how to remember her name, I see."

"Sonia just rolls off the tongue better."

"Ma, you alive up there?" Mecca's voice rang out from the first floor. "I was knocking but you didn't answer."

"Don't tell me that's the spoiled teenager I hear," came Lindsey's awed tone from across the line.

"Are you as surprised as I am?" Traci asked, turning her

attention to Mecca making her way up the stairs. "Girl, why were you making all that noise and scaring me like you don't have your own key?"

"I'm sorry. They're down in my bag and it's cold outside. Are you on the phone?"

"Oh, that's just your father." Traci spoke into the receiver again, ready now to be conciliatory. "I promise not to strangle her, Lindsey. If she shocks me again and gets this diploma, I'll even be nice to your friend what's-her-name when you visit in June. Gotta go, bye!" And she hung up before he could respond. Mecca's reply was more than enough.

from WHAT THE WOLF WANTS

ASHLEY BLOOMS

Esther had never truly known a home. She barely remembered the house she had lived in for the first seven years of her life, though she dreamed of it sometimes. Always of the willow tree by the kitchen whose roots had broken through their floors and taken over their garden, fighting them at every turn to reclaim the land. Just before they left, Esther's mother took an axe to the tree in the middle of the night, leaving it mangled but still standing. It was the last thing Esther ever saw of home, and she couldn't help but think that somehow, it was her fault. She carried the image of the tree's contorted limbs with her wherever she went—the split bark peeled back to reveal the tender flesh inside, paler because the light had never touched it.

She had been seven when they left that home, and it seemed to unlock something in her parents. They could never get enough leaving after that. The rest of her childhood was a blur of front doors and cracked foundations, leaking roofs and creaking floors, messy goodbyes and half-buttoned coats, and always, always, hurried escapes. A decade had passed since that first move, but Esther found that each move still felt the same.

They had only been in the house she stood in for eight months, but the leaving had found them again, hurried onward by the angry men outside their front door.

"When will they go away?" Esther's little sister, Mary, asked their mother. Mary crouched by Esther's knee, digging a hole into the hardpacked earth with the sharp end of a hair pin. The cellar they hid in had been half-built when they moved into the house. Even empty, the space was still too small for the three of them to fit side-by-side, so they curled into themselves as best they could.

"They will tire soon," their mother said. "They always do. And then they will leave."

Esther stared at the roots that poked through the earthen walls of the cellar just beside her cheek. She couldn't imagine what plant they might belong to, perhaps something as delicate as the roots themselves—a tiny, trembling thing, too small, even, to be green. But still, as small as it must be, the plant had survived, and sent its roots seeking water until they met the end of the earth and pushed further, out into open air where they could tickle Esther's cheek. She wished she could offer the roots something more than just her skin. She wished to open her mouth and let them drink from her. An offering—one body to another. At least then the plant would know what it was like to feel full.

The roots shook in tandem with the front door overhead, the wood beaten beneath the fists of angry men shouting Esther's father's name. Esther hadn't seen her father in weeks aside from envelopes of money he sent from time to time, each of them growing thinner than the last. Dirt fell onto Esther's shoulders, and she stifled a sneeze.

"What did Papa do this time?" Mary asked.

"Maybe he feigned suicide again," Esther said.

Mary frowned. "He promised he wouldn't do that anymore."

"Maybe it was jewels then. He always wanted to try that." Esther let the roots graze the thin skin of her eyelids. She shivered. "Or perhaps it was land this time. He said he may sell that cave, remember?"

"What cave?" Mary asked.

"Oh, it doesn't exist, really. More of an idea than a cave." Esther leaned back. She chewed on the inside of her cheek. "What I wonder is why they came here."

Mary shrugged. "Because they are looking for father."

"Yes, but father hasn't been here for months. He would have found residence somewhere else by now. So why would the men come here to look for him?"

Esther eyed their mother. She must have asked herself the same question, and she must have thought of the same answers. At best, Esther's father had gotten sloppy and let the address slip, either in conversation or in evidence, and the men had tracked him down. Or—and Esther knew, somehow, in her heart, that this was the more likely option—he had used this address as a decoy. He led the men here, knowing that they would find nothing but a house full of women, assuming they would turn around and go home and cut their losses, but he had been wrong, as he so often was.

"Your father is a very clever man. He has a reason for everything," their mother said. "If he were here…" She clutched her hands against her lower belly and closed her eyes.

Esther sighed. She had believed her father clever once, too, but he was growing careless. They left the last town on the run from the angry owner of the boarding house. The only thing that had saved them was the fact that Esther had grown close to the owner's daughter—a pretty, red-haired girl that loved to kiss the freckles on Esther's shoulders. She'd made Esther promise to write, then distracted her father with a fainting spell while Esther and her family fled.

At least then they had all been together. Now her father couldn't even do them the courtesy of seeing his ploys through to the end. Esther had tried to tell her mother as much, to help her make a new plan, to find a different way of surviving, but her mother would hear nothing of it.

Esther tried to focus on the roots instead of the bitterness in her stomach. At first, she'd thought the thin strands all came from the same source, but the closer she looked, the more she doubted that. It seemed that the roots had joined with other roots and tangled themselves into a knot—seeking desperately for what they needed, stretching out into the dark, reaching, hoping, until all they could find was each other. Sadness welled up in Esther, and anger, too.

She closed her eyes as, outside, the men grew quiet.

Mary smiled. "Maybe they're leaving."

Esther frowned. "Or maybe they're fetching an axe."

Their mother looked like she might reproach Esther, but then she nodded, slightly, to the cellar door beside Mary. A shadow fell between the cracks in the wood as one of the men walked by, seeking another entrance to the locked house. "Did you cover the door?"

Esther nodded. The cellar had been their fallback plan from the first moment they'd stepped into the rental. They'd built a trap door inside the house so they might have a place to hide if the time came for hiding, then repaired and covered the door leading outside if the time came for running.

One of the men shouted, "Enough of this, Callahan. Come out here and handle this like a man."

"Who's Callahan?" Mary whispered.

"Papa," Esther whispered back. "He used a fake name."

The men grew quiet before the same voice yelled again, "All right. You leave us no choice then. We're calling for the Sheriff."

The girls looked at their mother. Angry men could be avoided, disgruntled wives guilted into silence, but the Sheriff was another thing entirely. They'd always left town after one of her father's scams had gone wrong, long before the authorities could get involved, which is why Esther had known a dozen homes in her eighteen years.

But in all that time, they'd never been caught, never charged. They'd never even come close until recently. Esther wasn't sure what they would do if the men flung open the cellar and found them hiding there. If Esther was on her own, she wouldn't be worried about this. She wouldn't have to deal with her father reusing old tricks and old names, tripping over his own lies, or her mother's constant denial of their precarity. The thought had occurred to her more often as of late. She didn't have to stay.

Though she had nowhere to go, either. Had her parents been of a different station, she might have had more options. But all either of them had built in this life was either fake or fleeting. Esther had nothing to fall back on, no relatives to take her in, no hope for survival beyond marriage or charity or scheming herself. But standing there in the damp cellar, crowded between her mother and sister while angry men beat at their door, she thought her chances alone might be better after all.

The man outside the cellar door hollered for a lantern. He said, "I think there's something back here."

"Mama?" Esther asked.

Her mother's eyes were closed. She was so still that Esther might have believed she was praying, but her mother had stopped praying three months ago when their little brother, Edward, was born silent and tinged blue. They hadn't gone near the church since then or near the cemetery, either, not after the flood, and there'd been no mention of Grace or God or any holy thing. Something in her mother had shifted after Edward's death. Where her gaze had once been fixed solely on her family, it was suddenly wandering and unfocused. Her optimism soured and her faith wavered. She seemed to shrink into herself like a flower blooming in reverse, plunging itself into the ground, seeking shadows instead of sunlight.

"Mama," Esther repeated, more firmly this time, meaning to infuse the words not with a question, but a direction: *you are our mother, and you must act like it.* "We have to go."

"Where?" Mary whispered.

Their mother's eyes opened suddenly, as though she'd had a revelation. "Wait here," she said. She shimmied up the trap door that led into the main room of the house.

Esther said, "Do you think she'll start a fire?"

Mary stood and tucked her hair pin, now pitifully bent, back into the mess of her curls. "But she started a fire last time."

"And the time before that," Esther said. "It's the only trick she knows. Though, I suppose if it works, you only need one."

After a moment, a man near the front door shouted, "I saw him! I saw him move! He's in there, all right, I told you!" The shadow that had lingered by the cellar door moved away.

"Catch," their mother whispered from above, and Mary had just enough time to hold out her arms before a satchel dropped through the trap door, followed quickly by two more and then their mother's shadow descending on them like nightfall. She was panting softly when she landed in the cellar, her cheeks flaming pink, and she seemed more alive than she had since Edward died. She closed the trap door behind her, and it was so cleverly designed that it would take the men a few minutes to find it and realize that they'd been fooled. By then, Esther and Mary and her mother would be gone.

"Will we come back?" Mary asked, planting herself in front of the cellar door so her mother couldn't reach for the handle.

"Mary," their mother said. "Now is not the time."

"It's a simple question, isn't it? Will we come back home?"

"This isn't our home," their mother said.

"Then where is?"

Outside, the men began to shout to each other, calling for an axe or a shovel, anything to break the door down. The thick, acrid scent of burning was beginning to fill the house, and it tickled the back of Esther's throat.

"Our home is here," their mother said. "With each other."

Mary's hands curled into fists at her sides.

"Listen," their mother said, her voice carefully concealing the panic Esther could sense in her every movement. "If we can make it out of this cleanly, with no trouble, we'll be able to stay longer at the next house. Settle down for a while. Find a dog."

Mary's eyed widened. "Really?"

"Yes." Their mother beamed at Mary. "Yes, of course. But only if we can get out of here quickly. Can you do that for me?"

Esther's stomach curled. Her mother had made the same promise to her once, years before, and a thousand promises like it. In some warmer place, there was a version of Esther with a pet and a garden full of irises and no more fighting, no more lying, no more running.

And just like Esther had believed their mother, Mary did, too. Their mother kissed Mary's cheek three times and took hold of her hand as, outside, the men began to beat the door with what sounded like a hammer—one loud, percussive bang after the other until the wood started to splinter. The noise was enough to conceal their departure and then some, so their mother gave one great push and the cellar door swung open, revealing the dark night sky.

Mary was the first through the door and into the narrow alley behind the house, then their mother, but Esther lingered just a moment longer. She twined her finger around the roots, tracing the place where they had joined together, and as her mother bent down and hissed her name, Esther tore the roots apart. Then she was gone, up the narrow steps and out into the cool September air just as the men breached the doorway and stumbled into the smoking house.

There weren't many roads to the east, and none of them were safe for Esther and her family to travel, so they walked through the woods instead. Soon, the shadows of town faded, and the distant voices of angry men were swallowed by whippoorwills calling back and forth across the trees. The world grew quiet and soft beneath the full light of the moon. The further removed from danger, the slower Esther walked, her whole body sinking after the rush of their escape. The decision to leave her family sat like an anchor in her stomach.

She had left a dozen lives behind already. She knew exactly what to do. But the thought of leaving her family made her mind blank and cold. No plan sprang forth, no lies rushed to her lips. Just quiet, and something like sadness.

It was not just that she couldn't imagine what her life would look like. Where would she go, how would she survive, what would she become—but she couldn't imagine answering any of those questions without Mary or her mother.

Esther crossed into a stand of pines, the ground going soft beneath her feet from a blanket of fallen needles. Their mother pulled a soft blue blanket from her satchel and draped it over her neck like a scarf. Edward was meant to be buried in the blanket, but at the last moment, their mother had changed her mind. She couldn't part with the thing that had swaddled him after birth, so he had been buried with one of their father's shirts instead.

Their mother worried at the threads of the blanket until she eventually pulled one loose and used her teeth to bite it into a smaller piece. She wrapped the thread—as thin and blue as Edward's lips had been—around a branch and tied it swiftly in a knot, then kept walking as though nothing had happened. She repeated the gesture over and over, leaving scraps of Edward's blanket under heavy stones by the bank of a stream, tied round the waist of saplings no higher than Esther's knee, and sometimes dropped gently from her palm where they floated like seeds searching for soil to plant themselves in, like a little piece of Edward might sprout there in the morning.

The night Edward was born, Esther's father had left home not long after her mother's water broke, taking Mary with him because he said she was too young to hear her mother's screams. He had promised to call for a midwife on his way and left before there could be any questions. Esther had stood silent as the door slammed shut behind them, some part of her wondering when she had outgrown the right to be protected from terrible things.

Then her mother had begun to pant and groan.

In her dreams of Edward, Esther was always alone in a blue-lit forest, and she could hear her brother crying from beneath piles of damp leaves and dark soil, and she would start digging, her fingernails bending and breaking away, her knuckles raw and bloody, her body sinking deeper and deeper into a wood with no end as Edward fell silent.

Ever since that night, their mother had sworn that she could still feel Edward near her. Sometimes she heard him crying in the walls or felt the phantom weight of a small foot on the inside of her ribs. She spoke to him when she thought she was alone, though Esther had never been able to make out the whispered words.

Their family had lost so much over the years. Money had come and gone like rainfall, friendships sundered, favorite dresses and books and toys left behind in hurried exits, but Edward's loss bit deeper than the rest. It lingered.

Now Esther meant to leave, too. To become just another wound for her family to heal around, sealing themselves tighter than ever before over her absence. She couldn't break their hearts that way, not until she knew that they were safe. She would leave only once she was sure that Mary and her mother had a plan of their own.

Their mother ripped another string from the blanket and wrapped it around her finger. Mary stopped walking and asked her what she was doing.

"It's silly," their mother said. "But we left so quickly, and he was so small when.... I just want him to know where we're going. I want him to find us again."

Mary nodded as though it were the simplest thing in the world. She hooked her arm around their mother's and gave her a tight squeeze before she held out her hand. Their mother hesitated before placing a thin blue string inside. Mary walked ahead and tied the string to the tallest branch that she could reach, but not before placing a kiss to the thread so Edward would know that she welcomed him, too. After a moment, Esther joined them, and the three passed the night that way, carefully making a path through the woods for their little ghost.

Esther toyed with the smoldering ashes of their fire the next morning as Mary wandered around the campsite, both waiting for their mother to return with breakfast. The sun had not yet broken through the clouds and the woods still slept around them. Only the birds stirred, drawing lazy circles around the tops of the trees like they meant to crown them.

"Esther?" Mary called. "Come look."

"I don't want to see another caterpillar, Mary."

"It's not a caterpillar. It's a wolf."

Esther's chest tightened. "That's not funny."

Mary didn't answer.

"Mary?"

Esther gritted her teeth as she rose still holding a twig in her hand. She gripped it tightly, knowing Mary just wanted attention, but part of her was scared all the same. She rounded the wide trunk of a maple and found Mary standing a few feet away, her hand pressed to a faded piece of paper pinned to the trunk of a tree.

Esther tossed the twig at Mary's shoulder, and it bounced lightly to the ground. "You might have mentioned it was a drawing."

"There's no fun in that," Mary said. "What do you think this means?"

Esther stood behind Mary's shoulder and read the faded print. Their mother had taught Esther to read when she was a girl, and she had helped teach Mary to read in turn. It was one of the few things their mother demanded for them in terms of education, and one of the things Esther felt most grateful for. Esther read, "For the destruction of property in excess of $3,000. See James Whiting, Clover."

"How can a wolf do that much damage?" Mary asked.

"Killing. They hunt cattle and little sisters."

Mary frowned. "Don't tease me."

Esther trailed her fingers over paper. A faded image of a wolf stalked across the center, its body low to the ground, its open mouth full of jagged teeth. Esther's own teeth seemed terribly small and flat by comparison, her own eyes much weaker than the wolf's. She felt a flare of jealousy.

Their mother trundled through the trees behind them. She was breathing hard, her cheeks flushed with color, with the pale blue of Edward's blanket draped loosely across one shoulder. She smiled as she let loose of the skirt she had gathered in her hands. A dozen stunted apples fell to the ground and rolled across the damp grass.

"Eat up," she said. "And save what we don't finish. There's still much road to travel."

"How much road?" Esther asked. "You never said where we were going."

"Look mama," Mary said, pointing at the wolf.

Their mother ignored Esther and walked to Mary's side, reading the paper through squinted eyes. She frowned as she reached the bottom and said, "It almost seems an omen."

"Why?" Esther asked.

"Because that's where we're headed," their mother said. "To Clover."

Esther's stomach dropped. She had been so focused on escaping that she hadn't considered that where they might run to was worse than what they left behind. "You don't mean…"

"Yes," their mother said without looking at her. "We're going to Aunt Martha's."

"Who is Aunt Martha?" asked Mary.

"You've met her before," their mother said. "But you might've been too small to remember. Esther could tell you."

Esther bristled. "I'd rather not."

"Why?" Mary asked.

"We went there during a difficult time." Their mother kicked dirt atop their fire to choke the last vestiges of flame. Dark smoke billowed around her ankles. "Aunt Martha helped us through it as she's helped me through all my troubles. We came out of it a stronger family."

"Did we?" Esther asked.

Esther had been seven when she went to Aunt Martha's house. It was the first time she'd ever moved and the only move that didn't come because of her father's lies, but because of what happened with Esther's uncle. She didn't like to remember those days, and neither did her mother. No one in the family spoke of what happened and they didn't speak Esther's uncle's name, either. It was as if that time didn't exist, except inside Esther.

"You never gave Martha's a chance," their mother said. "You hated it from the start. We were lucky Martha was so patient. You were a beast in those days, angry at everything. You uprooted her flower beds, destroyed your clothes, screamed in the middle of the night."

Memories of those days at Martha's swarmed in Esther throat, heavy and stinging—small hands ripping a neat row of flowers from their bed, her favorite nightgown torn to tatters, a room full of windows. But all this paled in comparison to what happened at the church near Martha's home. It had been Easter. The pews had been filled with happy strangers and Esther had felt out of place in her dress. She could still hear the creak of the large wooden doors swinging open in the middle of the pastor's sermon. Every head had turned as Esther's uncle barged inside and shouted her name, demanding to see her.

"Why was that, mother?" Esther asked. "Why was I such a terror?"

Her mother paled. "Martha's is the safest place for us now."

"Why can't we find a boarding house instead?" Esther asked. Her vision felt momentarily narrowed, like she was looking at the world from the end of a long, dark tunnel.

"With what money?" their mother asked.

Esther resisted the urge to snatch an apple from her hands. "We can work then. We have before."

"What about father?" Mary asked.

"How will he know we're at Martha's?" Esther raised her hands and dropped them against her sides.

"Because that's where we've always agreed to go in case of emergency. He will know to meet us there. He will write or he will come. And until he does, we will wait for him." Their mother stared at Esther for a moment before turning back to Mary. "Besides, there is no better place than Martha's. She has a garden and a big farmhouse. She lives alone with her housekeeper now that her husband's passed. She's a very smart woman. And kind. She always took care of me, long before I knew how to care for myself."

Their mother ignored Esther's anger and continued her story, which made the house sound like something from a fairy-tale, a golden land where little girls were safe, and women were cherished. Aunt Martha was all but sainted in their mother's memories, but in Esther's mind she was a large woman with a dark brow who rarely spoke. Her presence loomed like a shadow over Esther's shoulder, watching her like a lit fuse that must be extinguished at every moment.

"You forgot to mention how strange her house is," Esther goaded. She was angry at her mother's baseless optimism, angry at being led back to Aunt Martha's when it was the seat of so many bad memories, and angry at herself for not leaving her family sooner. But Esther had no way of saying this, no way of speaking the truth without bringing up what had happened to her, and she couldn't bear to do that, so all she had left were petty jabs and needling. "All the children in Clover tell stories about Aunt Martha's house around the fire at night."

Their mother frowned. "It's a different sort of home. People aren't used to it."

"Different how?" Mary asked.

"You'll just have to see," their mother said. "You can't describe Aunt Martha's house, really. You must be in it for yourself, and you will be as soon as a I find a ride. I passed a farmhouse on the way. Come now, let's hurry."

It was long past dark by the time the farmer dropped them at the end of Aunt Martha's drive, and later still when they finally saw Aunt Martha's house in the distance. It sat at the end of a long, narrow dirt road, surrounded on two sides by a thick wood. Esther searched the road and the woods for signs of light or life but found nothing. It had been a decade since she last walked this road, but surely there were people left in Clover who had been there that day in the church. People who would know Esther's family, and Esther herself.

The clouds had long covered the moon and everything around them had fallen to shadow, except Aunt Martha's house. Even from so far away, the white siding seemed to glow. The house made its own kind of light, like all day the wood had been storing up the sun and was releasing it in a faint, steady hum that Esther swore she could feel in her bones. The house was two stories and had a small porch in front with a square turret rising above it. The many dark windows looked even darker compared to the house's ghostly glow.

"It hasn't changed," their mother said, and smiled a little flickering smile that brightened her face for a moment before it faded, like just seeing the house had imbued her, for a moment, with its shine.

"I'd still rather be at home," Mary said.

Their mother sighed. "Home isn't safe anymore. Home doesn't have any family left inside. Home doesn't have Lucy, either."

"Lucy?" Mary said. Then, "Lucy! Oh, Lucy lives in Clover! In town! Oh, can we go see her tomorrow? Please can we visit?"

Their mother laughed. "We can't go visiting a lady in the shape we're in. We'll see her soon enough. I promise."

Their mother had known Lucy's mother since childhood. They'd both grown up in Clover and became close friends even though Lucy's family came from wealth and Esther's mother did not. The two had kept up through letters and had decided that their two youngest daughters should be friends as well. As soon as Lucy and Mary could write, they began to send letters to each other, which made Lucy Mary's oldest friend even though they had never met.

"This is wonderful," Mary said as she did a little hop. "Just wonderful. Everything will be better now, with a friend. And a dog, too! Lucy can help me name it. She loves every sort of animal. She's a botanist, you know, or she will be, one day. Oh, I'm so excited!"

Esther frowned as Mary clasped her arm and used it to spin herself in a circle. Mary had asked to stay almost everywhere they'd lived, professing a great and tender love for the boarding house crowded with strangers and smelling of sweat and the tiny shack they'd stayed in with the holes in its roof and mice nesting under their shared bed. Mary could fall in love with anything with a foundation. She was like a mountain born to a flock of ravens, and they were always tearing her up and carrying her away, and each move eroded a little more until standing there that night, she looked like a hill at best. Small and resolute, her narrow chin held up to the sky, determined to be happy at last.

Mary ran ahead and looped her arm around their mother's. They put their heads together, talking and laughing, all the bitter feelings from before suddenly melted away. Esther slowed her step. She used to play a game when she was little where she'd fall behind her mother when they were out walking and wait to see how far ahead her mother would get before noticing that Esther was gone. She liked the way her mother would pale and shout her name when she turned and couldn't see Esther. She liked the feeling of being missed. It seemed she could never get enough of it, for as soon as she felt it, the feeling faded, and she needed to be reminded again and again. She had hidden at Aunt Martha's, too. Once a day, at least, though often more. She'd learned every inch of the house, all the places no one else could fit. She'd followed her mother behind the walls and looked up at her through the floorboards as her dress swished around her ankles, holding back laughter, or sometimes tears. Her mother tired of this, of course, and the more Esther hid, the longer it took her mother to notice she was missing. At some point she'd stopped noticing all together.

And that night, looking at Mary and her mother, it seemed like Esther had never been there at all. There was no space for her cloudy moods and rude language in this new home of friendship and gardens and happiness.

All the better then that she would be leaving soon. Esther

took a deep breath and headed down the road again, though she refused to hurry her step or attempt to catch up.

Aunt Martha's house seemed dimmer from the porch, which was barely large enough to fit two rocking chairs side-by-side. The banister was peeling, the white paint curled back to reveal a flaxen blue beneath. Flower beds lined the edge of the porch, the soil gone fallow in the approaching cold. Now only a few twigs and sticks remained. An image came to Esther—small hands ripping a neat row of flowers from the bed. Her mother must have been right. Esther must have torn the flowers apart. She had been so angry back when she first came to Martha's, so full of bile. The skin on her palms itched and she could almost feel the flowers pulling at the root, the futile resistance of something trying to stay within its home.

Esther reminded herself that she would not be in this house for long. A few days, a week at most, just enough to see her family into Aunt Martha's hands, where they would be safe enough for Esther to leave them without guilt.

Her mother knocked and knocked again. They waited for a light to appear through the window. For voices calling out, hoarse and tired. For the creak of the door opening.

But Aunt Martha never came. The windows of the house stayed dark. The night sounds grew louder around them.

So, her mother kept knocking.

And as she did, Esther noticed what she had been too tired to notice before. The front porch was empty of anything, even a rocking chair or a rake for the leaves. And in the yard, grass had begun to grow up the narrow path that led to the front porch like it had been a while since anyone walked it. And there, just below her mother's hand, was a notice like the one they'd seen in the woods. This notice had no picture of a wolf, only text describing the damage the creature had done, but the paper was worn and yellowed and torn in several places.

After a while their mother stopped knocking and took a step back.

"She isn't here, is she?" Esther asked.

"No," their mother said. "I don't think she is."

Esther closed her eyes. She could feel every mile they had walked that day, every inch of ground they had covered, and the distance unfurled inside her until there was room for little else.

"What do we do now?" Mary asked.

Their mother sighed and put her hands on her hips. "What we must."

"Why am I always the one breaking into things?" Esther asked as she stared up at the window.

Mary knelt in the grass before Esther's feet and sighed. "Because you love it."

Esther grinned. "I do."

Aunt Martha had no visible neighbors, but Esther still insisted on going around the side of the house where no one could see them from the empty road. Esther climbed atop her sister's back and felt a pang of sadness. She'd climbed onto her father's back this way a few years before and broken into a widow's bedroom while a dinner party took place downstairs. And she'd climbed onto her mother's back as a girl to reach for a jewelry box as her father occupied the owner in the next room. Esther never liked to draw attention to herself, but she didn't mind doing things no one else saw. She was happiest in the shadows, behind closed doors, in empty corners, and her family always found a way to give her that.

Esther had tried to share these stories once, to the girl at the boarding house, lying in tall grass outside her bedroom window, tipsy on her father's secret liquor. Esther had cupped her hand over her mouth to stifle her laughter, but the girl had not laughed with her. She'd looked shocked, concerned, even a little afraid. And Esther hadn't known how to tell her that there was nothing to fear. That her family was never more a family than in those moments. And she didn't know how she could ever hope to be loved by someone who couldn't understand that.

"Stop sight-seeing and open the window," Mary growled beneath her.

Esther smiled and pried her fingers under the edge and forced the frame up. She slung her leg over and ducked her head beneath the glass as quickly as she could.

"What do you see?" Mary asked.

Esther's fingers trailed over the windowsill and cut a line through weeks of dust. The house had been empty for a while. As the details of the room emerged before her, Esther waited for another memory to surface like it had on the porch, but nothing did. The house was just a house. Nothing more.

Esther pulled back the curtains so the moon could light her path. All the furniture had been draped with heavy white cloths, which made the room look like a forest downed with snow. Even the mirrors and clocks on the walls had been hidden. Esther approached a long, low shape and pulled back the corner to find a handsome sofa in soft yellow-green fabric. There was a small table in the room and two armchairs, several oil lamps clustered together in the corner. Two rocking chairs flanked the fireplace and a large rug covered most of the floor, dampening the sound of Esther's footsteps. It was a soft room made softer by all the fabric draped around it. The kind of place where one would sit in quiet with their sewing in their lap, shielded from the cold and dark and danger of the world.

Martha had been lucky. Of all the ways that a woman could survive—charity, marriage, employment, crime—Martha had found a quiet, decent, wealthy man to marry. Her whole life had been changed by it.

Esther traced her finger along the mantel above a large fireplace, stirring more dust. She expected to find little trinkets atop the wood alongside samples of Aunt Martha's beading, a pretty snuffbox or ostrich feathers, but instead, a small animal skull rested in the center, the bone gleaming white in the darkness, alongside a string of dried acorns, and several thin books with blank covers.

The parlor led into a small foyer. To her left was the front door and to her right was a staircase that led to the second floor. Esther was tempted to explore the house while she was alone, but her mother and sister were waiting, and they would not wait quietly for long. She reached for the front door when something dark moved in the corner of her eye. She turned quickly but found only herself, reflected.

The walls of the foyer were covered in mirrors of all different shapes and sizes. The largest was an oval with a thin gilt frame, and the smallest barely the size of Esther's thumbprint with a delicate, ornate framework of brass surrounding its small surface. The mirrors had been fitted into place so carefully that it seemed they almost emerged from the walls naturally, like moss growing over a rock. Esther turned to the side and watched herself turn in two dozen directions, each version of her offering a slightly different view.

But she couldn't help but feel that not all the reflections had moved with her.

Something felt slower in the glass. Like parts of her were struggling to catch up. Esther took a step forward, toward the mirrors, and watched herself step forward, too, as though the two halves of her might meet. Even in the dim light from the windows, she cast a faint shadow behind her. Esther stepped forward again, and each image of her moved, except for one. In the largest mirror, with the thinnest frame, Esther's shadow didn't move with her. It stayed hunched in place, heavy as the moon.

And, as she watched, the shadow grew dark and darker.

Its round edges seemed almost to ripple, like something inside the shadow was rapidly outgrowing itself. It grew to Esther's knee, her hip. It started to unfurl at her elbow, the shape of it thinning, lengthening. It seemed almost on the verge of standing up.

Then something thumped upstairs. Loud and heavy, yet muffled, like a stone falling onto thick carpet. Esther jumped, and the reflection was broken. When she looked back at the mirror her shadow was only a shadow again.

CAESARA PITTMAN,
OR A NEGRESS OF GOD

MAURICE CARLOS RUFFIN

"Do you, Miss Caesara Pittman, in the year of our Lord eighteen hundred and sixty-six, aver to tell the truth, the whole truth, and nothing but the truth?" Davidson, the attorney of the City of New Orleans, asks. It's hot outside and hot in the courtroom. Too hot for so many people to be on those benches, close as piglets on a mama pig's teats.

I touch the Good Book, my fingers touching on the gold edges. That man, Buford—now I know his family name—sits at the table by his own lawyer, who wears those round glasses. Buford's eyes wide with hate. He making all kind of faces at me. With those stitches down his cheek, looks like his Lucifer hisself. But this book never sent me wrong. I place my hand on my left breast.

"Yessuh, I do," I say. "I promise on my very heart."

"Where were you on the evening of Wednesday, July 24, 1866?" Davidson rests his hands behind his back, making his belly stick out some. He's more than a couple of feet away. But I smell talc and pipe tobacco every time he pass by.

"As you say, mister. It was Wednesday, and I was down on Good Children Street to buy baguettes. I make bread pudding for my husband and young ones on Saturdays."

"On Saturdays?" Davidson's curled mustache shakes.

"You got to let it stale up good before you use it."

"Of course." Davidson laughs. Some of my folk in the gallery laugh good, too.

"It was long about sunset…" I wasn't far from home, had a basket on my arm. Had left the butcher where I cut offal for other free Creoles like myself. Had just passed the barn where they keep the streetcar mules when footsteps made themselves known to me. Some girls had been handled wrong lately. And some of them had been shamefully desecrated.

"I didn't come down here for no Devil work," I said, hoping to be heard. A man came out the shadow. Under the gaslight, this white man wore the clothing of a man of God. A white collar around his neck. A cross hanging underneath that.

"Just taking note of one of our Father's children." In the light, he rubbed his hands like he was cold.

But he had big shoulders and big, rough grabbing hands. The kind of hands that plowed soil or worked a cargo ship. Not the kind of hands that prayed over the sick or baptized little ones. I held my hand out, palm up. "You ain't no kind of priest."

He smiled, all the yellow teeth in his mouth shining at me. Looked like a mouth full of kernels.

"I don't take offense in the ignorance of your kind none," he said. And I wondered if I was wrong about who he might be. But I thought on the book and words came to my mouth.

And I saith: "Take no part in the unfruitful works of darkness, but instead expose them."

"What?"

"I rebuke you!" I knew enough to know that a priest should have got a twinkle in his eye when you said the Scripture to him. But this heathen's eyes stayed black. He might as well have been deaf. I dropped my basket and ran. I was fast but got tangled in my skirts. Fell on those cobblestones. Hurt my wrist.

He fell on top me, clawing at my clothes. Pushed me on my back. He pulled at my chignon. That made me madder than what I already had reason to be mad about. He shouldn't have done it. But, the exacerbated madness reminded me of the poultry knife I kept in my hair. I bought my manumission five years before the war. I was a free woman, but that didn't mean I didn't have to prove it from time to time. When slave traders needled me, I had my papers in one hand and my shiny little knife in the other.

This man's sick breath was on my face, and he was yanking my skirt. So, I jugged that knife in right under his left eye and drug it down to his lip. I smelled the metal that's in blood. He yowled like a pitiful li'l dog. If I would have drug up instead of down, I could have popped his eyeball out like a—

Davidson raises his arm. "Thank you, Miss Pittman. That will do enough. We do not wish to give the jury night terrors."

I huffed.

"What about my terrors?" I say, but he don't hear.

Davidson points at Buford. "Is this the man who accosted you?" Buford still making faces. He ugly as a pot of chitlings. His outside match his insides. I like that I did that to him.

Outside the courtroom window, the paddleboat toots. I watch a colored man throw bread at a duck. Some changes done happened since the war between the states. I was a slave most of my life working the house on a plantation up near St. Francisville. I ain't a slave no more, but I know these people in the juror box. Few of them would have wished any of us found freedom. Mr. Barker with the ruddy red cheeks sells candles and other fine things. The man with the mutton chops runs carriages. The dandy one on the end is from Virginia, almost a carpet-bagger. Virginians used to sell my people to New Orleans for punishment. They hoped heat and terror work would kill us all. And then there's all the marching men the so-called police killed at the convention not long after my meeting with Buford. The whites trapped the good men inside that Mechanics' Institute. When the men surrendered, dropping weapons, hands up, the so-called police murdered them anyway, right in the streets. Paul Dostie was holding a white flag when they shot him.

I expect no kind of justice here. I'm just another darky, hardly worth throwing away the life of one of their own, guilty or not.

So, we really only here on account of how loud Buford screamed when I cut him. Like a babe with the colic. They saw my clothes, shredded like I'd been clawed by a lion. And they saw Buford, too big around the shoulders and too rough around the hands to be a priest. The so-called police grabbed Buford on the spot. We made the papers. That's why we here. Because of all the attention.

"That man at that table over there?" I ask.

"Yes, miss," Davidson, the attorney of the City of New Orleans, says. "Have you seen him afore?"

"The man over there who's ugly as sin?" Some of my folk up the galley laugh again. But the men in the juror box are beet-faced.

"Miss Pittman, I must insist—"

I squint. "I never seen that man before in all my born life," I say. "I swear it." People all around the room gasp.

The judge bangs his gavel. Buford's lawyer with the round glasses stands.

"Your honor, I move for an immediate dismissal of the present matter."

Later, it's dark out. The bells of St. Louis Cathedral over Jackson Square ring out. This is how I know it's round midnight when Buford shows his face at the exit of the district jail. A so-called policeman shoves him out. Buford dusts off his coat and starts toward the cathedral. But he won't make it. I doubt he was going to pray to the Lord anyhow. Don't matter none. My basket is full of baguettes and oranges for my young ones. And I have a knife. A long one, too. I use it for gutting sow. When I pull it out, it shakes like it's singing. Don't matter if Buford was going to pray. I'm his Lord tonight.

from THE HOUSE UPTOWN

MELISSA GINSBURG

Prologue (1997)

Lane came awake to the sound of unoiled hinges, her heart pumping hard. She had been dreaming of a massive cloud, a storm that blew all the doors open, dread billowing around her. She struggled to wrench herself from the panic of the dream. The clock read 2:30. She inhaled deeply, lay still, willing her body to relax. She listened to the house settle, visualized her daughter Louise tucked safely in bed down the hall. Lane was almost back asleep when she heard a sound that shouldn't be there—footsteps? Voices? Lane's arms tingled, her heart pounded again. She sat up in bed, reached for the light, froze at the distinct soft thud of the kitchen door closing.

Swiftly Lane shoved her feet into slippers and went to the door, opened it, listened again. What was Louise up to, sneaking out in the middle of the night? Or sneaking in a boy? At seventeen, it was the age for those shenanigans. Lane would have to ground her, the whole house would be tense and awful, it would

WHAT WE ARE BECOMING

be impossible to get any work done. Lane thought of her upcoming deadlines—she was already behind schedule and this would make it worse. Irritation replaced the fear she had felt a moment ago.

She heard a voice again, coming from the kitchen. A man's voice. Who the hell was Louise mixed up with? She crept down the hall toward the kitchen, listening. The man spoke again, though she couldn't make out the words. She heard someone answer, not her daughter. Burglars. At least two of them.

She walked fast, careful to avoid the creaks in the old hardwoods. She made her way toward her daughter's bedroom at the front of the house. As she passed the mantel she grabbed a heavy brass candlestick, carried it at her side. She wished for a better weapon, but her gun was locked up in the hall closet, she'd never get to it in time. More important to get Louise away from them, out of the house.

She would wake Louise and they would run out the front door, it was the closest. Lane tried to remember if the key was in the lock, or in her purse—where had she left it? Her skin prickled everywhere, her grip tightened on the candlestick. She could still hear, faintly, the men in the kitchen.

She was almost to the front hall, almost to Louise, when she mis-stepped, hit the treads too hard. The floor creaked. The voices behind her stopped. Lane looked towards the kitchen. A man stepped into the hall, a shadowy bulk looming. He saw her. Too late to run. She turned towards him, ready to fight, to keep them away from her girl. A red rage obscured all thought. She lunged forward, raising the candlestick.

"Lane," he said.

It was Bertrand. Not a burglar. She lowered her arm. Her body sagged in relief.

He stepped into a pool of streetlight coming in the window and she saw the outline of his head, his familiar shoulders.

"Jesus, you scared me to death," she said. "I thought you were breaking in."

The adrenaline was still pumping through her. She forced herself to take a deep breath. She went to him, stepped into his embrace. She loved how their bodies fit together, loved to feel his breath in her hair. But he never came to her like this, in the middle of night, never when Louise was home.

"You shouldn't be here," she said.

"I'm sorry," he said. "I know."

"Who were you talking to?"

"Come in the kitchen. I need your help."

He took the candlestick from her hand and set it down. She smelled his sharp metallic sweat, sensed his tension. Lane followed him in and switched on the overhead.

A boy stood beside the kitchen table, younger than Louise. He flinched at the sudden light. He was skinny, tall, with a neat haircut. He was dressed in basketball shorts and a t-shirt, its silk-screened logo obscured with reddish brown stains. Dried blood flaked from his bare arms and legs. It was smeared across his forehead and one cheek where he must have rubbed his face. The boy stood there, trembling, looking at his puffy sneakers, expensive ones. One sock crusted in blood.

"This is Artie," Bertrand said. "My son."

Lane, astonished, stared at the boy. In all the years they'd been together, Lane had never met Bert's kids, had never wanted to. The boy's presence in her kitchen was a violation. She glanced around at the table piled with papers, the dishwasher door open, the calendar hanging on the wall by the phone, marked up with Louise's school events. Louise's physics textbook open on the counter next to Lane's sketches. Her eyes skittered back to the kid. He did not belong here. The light seemed to hit him differently.

"What is that," Lane said. "Is that blood?"

"It's not his," Bert said.

"Get him out of here," she said.

"Honey—" Bert said.

She turned and went back to her bedroom. Bert followed, still talking.

"This is an emergency, Lane. I wouldn't ask this if it wasn't."

"Take him home."

"I can't. Look, I have to deal with some things. Can you just keep an eye on him, get him cleaned up, find him something to wear?"

"But his mother—" Lane began.

"Lane. I can't. His sister's having a slumber party. Our house is full of eleven-year-old girls."

Our house. His and his wife's.

"Whose blood is that?" she said.

"Please, Lane. I need you."

"Answer me. What the fuck is going on?"

"I'll explain when I can. Just get him in the shower. Bag up his clothes. His shoes, too. Keep him here till I get back, don't let him leave. Don't answer the door—"

"Who the fuck is coming to the door?"

"No one. Just in case. Keep him out of sight, okay? Keep him hidden."

"Louise is here."

"I'm sorry," he said.

"Jesus, Bert," she said.

"We'll talk later," he said. "I promise." He was already turning away.

"Do not leave," she said. "Do not leave him in my house. Bert."

"I'll be back as soon as I can."

She followed him to the kitchen. He put his hand on the boy's shoulder and spoke to him.

"Artie, she's going to help us. Do what she says. I'll be back. I'm going to take care of everything."

The kid nodded.

"Good boy," Bert said.

Lane and the boy watched him leave. The boy uttered a stifled cry when his father shut the door behind him.

"Goddammit, Bert," Lane said.

The kid looked at her for the first time. He resembled his mother, Lane noted. She'd seen plenty of pictures of her in the society pages.

"Be quiet," Lane said. "Come with me, the bathroom's this way. Don't make a sound."

She turned to go but he didn't follow.

"Come on," Lane said.

He didn't move.

"Are you hurt?" she said, more gently.

He shook his head.

"What the hell happened to you?"

He opened his mouth as though to speak but let out a loud sob instead. Once he started he couldn't seem to stop.

"Hush," she said. "You have to be quiet."

But the kid was unable to control himself. His crying made Lane want to shake him.

"Forget it, don't think about it," she said.

She forced herself to reach out to him, and awkwardly patted his bloodied arm. "It's okay," she said. "Don't cry. You have to be quiet."

Gradually his sobs turned to loud hiccups, though his body still shook.

"That's better," Lane said. "Neither of us wants to be in this situation. Let's just get through it, alright? We'll get it over with. You are going to take a shower."

He nodded miserably and allowed her to guide him to the back bathroom. She showed him how to use the tricky old faucet, let the water run until it got hot.

"Get in," she said. "I'll go find you something to wear."

She left him there with the water running. She took a garbage bag from under the kitchen sink, then went to her bedroom to look through her clothes. The kid was skinny. He ought to be able to fit into something baggy. She found an old pair of paint-stained sweatpants and an oversized T-shirt. She knocked on the bathroom door. He didn't respond.

"Artie, I'm coming in, okay?"

She pushed the door open to find him standing there, still dressed, staring at his face in the mirror.

"Kid," she said. "Come on. Get undressed."

He was unresponsive, in shock or something. She'd never seen anything like it. She touched his shoulder, and he reacted—he gave a soft cry and his body crumpled inward. He moaned something unintelligible.

"What?" she said.

"I didn't mean to do it," he said, turning to her. His voice cracked, uneven and raw.

"Do what?" she said.

He shook his head.

"What did you do?"

"It was an accident."

"What was?"

He didn't answer. He shook his head like he was trying to dislodge some vision. He was trembling all over.

"Artie, don't think about it. Just get in the shower, alright?"

He made no move to get undressed.

"Kid, come on. We agreed, right? You have to get cleaned up."

He looked at her then.

"Who are you?" he said.

"Nobody," she said. "A friend of your dad's."

He looked, if possible, even more alarmed.

He was putting it together. He hadn't known. Bert should never have brought him here.

"I'm trying to help you," she said.

She shoved the clean clothes and the black garbage bag at him and he took them.

"Put everything of yours in this bag," she said.

"Don't—" his voice cracked again and he stopped.

"What?" she said.

"Don't leave me alone."

Jesus, she thought. She would never forgive Bert for this. The boy was going to break down again, start wailing at any second. He would wake up Louise and everything would get much, much worse.

"Alright, I'll be right here, right outside the door. I can leave it open a crack, how's that?"

Artie nodded. "Thank you," he said.

"Get undressed."

She left the bathroom, pulled the door halfway shut behind her. She heard him undress and put his clothes in the bag, pull the shower curtain aside, step under the water.

"I'm still right here, Artie," she said.

Lane turned to see a figure standing at the other end of the hallway, watching her against the light of the open bathroom door.

"Louise," Lane said. "How long have you been there?"

Chapter 1 (2017)

Ava was on a train called The City of New Orleans, on her way to the actual city of New Orleans, where her grandmother lived. She carried a backpack filled with books and a small suitcase of clothes. It was summer. She had finished the eighth grade four weeks before. Her mother had been dead for three. Louise had walked into the emergency room with a bad headache, and twenty hours later she was gone. A freak thing, the doctors said—a rare virus that attacked the brain stem.

Ava watched the green landscape flip past her train windows. She tried reading Harry Potter but she was too distracted, so she paced up and down the train cars. She'd never been anywhere besides her home in Iowa and one trip to Chicago. The country seemed too big. Ridiculously big.

Her mother's roommate Kaitlyn had driven her to meet the train in Chicago. The three-hour trip from Iowa City had been laced with Kaitlyn's endless stories about her boyfriend who may or may not have been flirting with his neighbor down the block, whom Kaitlyn described as "one of those overgrown Girls Gone Wild sluts, I mean, she's thirty years old for God's sake"; Kaitlyn's mother, who perpetually got on her nerves; and Kaitlyn and Louise's bitchy boss at the factory who had been unexpectedly kind when Louise got sick. It was easy to be with Kaitlyn because she never stopped chattering and did not require a response. Ava knew she was doing it on purpose, keeping things light. They'd been crying for weeks and needed a break. Ava was tired and numb, relieved to be away from the pity on everyone's faces, and all the places where her mother should have been.

Kaitlyn parked in front of the train station in Chicago and handed Ava a sheaf of twenty-dollar bills.

"Keep it in your bra," she said.

The girl gave her a look. Kaitlyn was always being embarrassing.

"Or your sock."

"Thank you," Ava said.

"I wish I could come with you," Kaitlyn said.

"It's okay. I'll be fine."

"Don't let anybody talk to you."

"Okay."

"People aren't good, remember that."

She'd heard Kaitlyn say this before, it was one of her maxims.

"I know," Ava said.

"Smart girl."

Ava got out of the car. A printout of her train ticket was in her jeans pocket, creased and sweaty from her anxious hand. Her grandmother in New Orleans had paid for the ticket. Ava watched Kaitlyn drive off before she went into the station, found her platform, and boarded the train. She tried not to think about the speed at which it carried her away from home.

The train arrived in the afternoon. Ava had grown up hearing stories of New Orleans her whole life, and was half-surprised, now, to find that it was a real place. So far it was dirtier and uglier than she had pictured, the train station far less impressive than the ornate one she'd left in Chicago.

Ava looked around for her grandmother. She wondered if there would be a sign with her name on it, maybe some balloons or flowers like in the movies, when people arrived somewhere. She walked from one end of the station to another, scanning faces, more black faces in one place than she had ever seen before. No old ladies stood around waiting for her. She bought a Coke from a machine. She studied the mural that stretched above the ticket counter, a depiction, it said on the wall, of the history of New Orleans. The paintings were violent and disturbing, with dark colors and sharp angular figures doing terrible things to one another.

After a while she went outside and stood under the broad awning. A jumble of freeway overpasses loomed next to the building. The heat was shocking, thick. She waited there, trying to guess what kind of vehicle her grandmother might own. She imagined a plump gray-haired lady and a plush sedan, a jar of cookies, a guest room. She sweated against her backpack and her suitcase felt heavy and slick in her hand. She went back in to the air conditioning.

Ava wandered around the station, past blue and brown chairs

bolted to the floor. She found a pay phone and tried Lane's number but it rang and rang. Ava waited through a series of buses unloading, each dispensing a throng of people into the station. She checked outside again. No luck.

Back inside she was pacing, too anxious to sit. People around her surged toward and away from buses, hugged and stretched and dragged their luggage. Ava went for the third time into the gift shop and studied the souvenir trinkets and t-shirts. The lady behind the counter spoke to her.

"Hey, babe, can I help you find something in particular?"

"No," Ava said. "Thank you. I'm waiting for my ride." She stood next to a shelf of real baby alligator heads. They'd been coated in some kind of shellac and they glistened under the fluorescent fixtures.

"You been waiting a while. Maybe they're not coming."

Ava said, "I was thinking that, too."

"Where you trying to go?"

Ava opened her backpack and found the little book where she had written down her grandmother's address. She read it out.

"Dang, that's way Uptown."

"Could you tell me how to get there?"

"You could maybe take the streetcar, if it's running," the woman said.

"What's the streetcar?" Ava asked.

The woman frowned. "Maybe better if you have money for a cab. You have money?"

Ava nodded.

"Go see if there's one out there."

Ava thanked the clerk and walked into the humid heat and car exhaust of the Central Business District. She approached a waiting cab and gave the driver the address. He helped her with her case and she got in the car. A television played flashy celebrity gossip news in the backseat and Ava watched it as they bumped over rutted streets.

Ava had never been in a taxi before, but this experience was no less strange than any of the past three weeks. After the hospital and the funeral, the world was not what she had thought. Things happened and she observed them with a detachment that overlay a deep, unaccessed horror. Just get there, Ava thought. See what happens next.

Chapter 2

Lane hunched over the sketchbook on the table, drawing in a rush of focused energy, like the world might end at any minute. Nothing mattered but the work, even if it was some bullshit commissioned piece for a stupid hotel she would otherwise never set foot in. Something distressing lived in a part of her mind she had no access to, but she caught glimpses of it sometimes. Slivers of trouble coming, or trouble already happened and forgotten but spreading its damage around, just beyond the edges of thought.

The day was still, the light in the kitchen soft and diffused. Lane knew the paths of the sunlight in every room of the house. As a girl she had watched the angles of sun and shadow until she had them memorized. Fifty, sixty-something years ago. Now the house was like an extension of her intelligence, a container of memories she mostly ignored as she sketched.

This mural, for a new restaurant in the Marigny, was to be a landscape extending across four walls of the large dining room. A traditional scene of the neighborhood when it was still part plantation and a few narrow cobblestone streets. They wanted authenticity, historical accuracy, photorealism—Lane's specialties. For weeks she'd been researching old maps and drawings.

She flipped through a book of costumes from the 1820s, marking pages of French and Haitian dress styles. She lost herself in the details, studying and sketching, until her physical reality brought her back to the kitchen. Stiff muscles, hunger, a headache that meant she needed caffeine. Crumbs on the table from breakfast cast tiny shadows indicating late afternoon. She stood and went to the refrigerator, poured a chicory coffee over ice, and lit the pipe that had gone out in the ashtray.

Lane heard a knock at the door, then the bell. She put down the pipe and went to answer. Caterers, the party, was that today? She must have written it down somewhere, on a notepad, but where was the notepad? She'd discovered in recent months that things had a way of proceeding on their own, even if she forgot all about them. People got alarmed when she asked questions or acted surprised, so she tried to project an air of benevolent nonchalance. She accepted whatever situation presented itself, as though she'd been expecting it. The marijuana helped.

But it wasn't the caterers, just a neighborhood boy selling buckets of popcorn for his soccer team. Lane sent him away and set out her large transferware platters for the party, even though it was her assistant Oliver's job. He would come over and organize everything, and they'd have a cocktail before the guests showed up. She depended on Oliver to see to all the small irritating details of her life so she could concentrate on her art. He'd worked for her for years now, since right after Katrina. She smoked some more, took a yogurt from the fridge. She hated having to eat. The dreary requirements of the body took up too much time.

When she was young, she'd devoted so much of her days to grocery shopping and cooking meals, trying out new recipes. She used to bake her own bread, when her husband Thomas was alive. Absurd to think of it now. Lane rarely thought about Thomas anymore. It had been nearly forty years since he'd died—a flash flood, his car hydroplaned and hit a truck. Could have happened to anyone. There had been the baby to deal with, and the problem of making a living, raising the child. She'd got on with it, put the marriage behind her.

Lately thoughts of Thomas tumbled into the present, unbidden. They felt like visitations of some sort, a transporting of the past into the present. A memory took over, a complete sensory immersion, paralyzing: the smell of yeast; the ringing phone; flour motes dancing through a shaft of kitchen sunlight; the cramp in her neck as she held the receiver with her shoulder to keep her hands in the dough. Flour handprint on the receiver, flour on her dress and in her hair.

Lane listened to the voice on the line. *Ma'am, you need to come down here.* She hung up, watched the long cord curling around itself. Thinking only, the bread will be ruined and·Thomas will complain. She would not have time to make more, what with the laundry, shopping, the other countless essential chores. But then she got ahold of herself. She covered the dough and put it in the icebox to stall the second rise, gathered up the baby, and drove to the hospital. When she got there she learned he was already dead.

She arrived home late that night, just her and little Louise. The dough had coated the outsides of the pans, having grown and bubbled up with yeast. The refrigerator was a mess, covered in dried dough. If she'd left right away, dropped the bread without a thought and rushed to his side, maybe he would have lived. If she'd been more kind-hearted, could she have seen him conscious once more? She could have been, one last time, the recipient of his gaze, full of love or disgust or whatever it was.

A month into young widowhood, she realized her days were less complicated than they had been before. Thomas had been too needy, like most men, unaware of the details that rendered their days seamless, the cooking and cleaning and errands. Men were so helpless. They couldn't even feed themselves. The baby sucked away at her, too, sapping her energy and time, but you could hardly blame a baby.

Lane experienced a sense of relief, immediate and astounding, when she learned the accident had killed him. She loved him, she wasn't a monster. But that first wave of clarity, that sense that she would be fine, that a lot of things would be easier now—she'd been right about that. She moved through her days quietly, caring for the baby, all the while listening to the rising sound inside her, a buzzing voice that grew more insistent. Her life was starting. It was all hers. She would never have to give it up again.

Oliver let himself in, carrying a case of wine and a bag from the art supply store. He closed the door with his foot and set the box down on the sideboard in the dining room. Lane was sitting at the big mahogany table. He saw the platters piled up at one end.

"What the fuck's all this out for?" Oliver said.

Lane glanced up from her sketchbook. "What?" she said.

He pointed to the platters. She'd quit throwing her monthly parties two years ago now.

Lane shrugged. "Wanted to look at that pattern. For a sketch."

"Huh. Would have thought it was the wrong period. This is late 1800s, isn't it?"

"You think these restaurant idiots know that?" Lane said.

Oliver laughed. "They'll sue you if they find out."

He touched the edge of the Limoges. It was Edwardian bone china, over a hundred years old, but the underside was chipped and the gilding mostly gone from the rim. Lane had run it through the dishwasher lord knows how many times, and it wasn't worth anything now. The house was crammed with used up, ruined treasures.

"Well," Oliver said, "do you need it still?"

"No."

She lit the pipe and handed it to Oliver. She was running low, he'd have to get her more soon. He smoked and handed it back, but she was drawing again, a picture of an old wall telephone with a cord. Obviously not for the restaurant project. He wondered about it but he had learned not to question Lane's process. She didn't think like ordinary people. You had to wait and see and then the end result was dazzling.

Oliver put the wine and art supplies away and carted the platters to the butler pantry where they belonged. He could see she was engrossed, and it was his job to protect her from any distraction. He went through the mail, tidied here and there, made a note she needed milk. As he worked he listened for signs that she was finishing up. Then he'd fix them Old Fashioneds, they could drink and talk. He'd make sure she ate something before he left for the night.

Chapter 3

Ava's cab parked in front of a wooden house, painted green. She paid and carried her bags to the front porch. The windows were leaded glass, wavy and old, distorting the reflection of the trees and telephone wires. Ava knocked.

After a minute a man opened the door. "Yes?" he said abruptly, irritation in his voice. He held a drink in his hand. Beyond him in the fading light were high ceilings, crown molding, Oriental rugs.

"Hi," Ava said. "Is this where Lane lives?"

"Who are you?" he said.

"I'm Ava. I'm her granddaughter."

"Bullshit," he said. "What's this about?"

"Is she here?" Ava said.

"You got ID or something?"

She shook her head. "I'm only fourteen." Kaitlyn's warnings about strange men echoed through her head. "Who are you?" she added.

"Wait here," the man said.

He closed the door, leaving Ava on the porch. After a minute he came back and opened it again. "You better come in, I guess," he said.

She lugged her case over the threshold. A woman stood in the middle of the room—graying hair pulled back in a ponytail, a paint-stained dress. She looked old enough to be a grandmother, but unlike any grandmother Ava knew. The woman stared openly at Ava.

"Louise," the woman said.

"No," Ava said. "I'm Ava. Are you Lane?"

"Lane, what the hell is going on?" the man said.

"God, you look like your mother," the woman said.

"Really?" Louise had been beautiful, and Ava thought herself plain, awkward.

"Okay, god," the man said. "Let's go sit down. I'm Oliver, by the way. I could use another drink."

Ava followed them through a living room, dining room, and a dark hall to a kitchen at the back. Lane sat down at a wooden table. On it lay a spiral sketchbook, an empty glass, an ashtray and small wooden pipe.

"What'll it be?" he said to Ava. "Diet Coke, water?"

"Water, please."

Lane spoke. "I haven't seen you in ten, eleven years."

"I don't remember it," Ava said. "I was too little, I guess."

"Yes," Lane said. "You've grown."

It was nearly dark out, the kitchen in shadows. Oliver switched on the light. He poured Ava a glass from the tap and fixed drinks for Lane and himself, brought everything to the table.

"Louise is dead," the woman said. She was speaking as though she had forgotten and suddenly remembered a piece of trivia.

"Yes." Ava said.

"That your mom?" Oliver asked.

Ava nodded.

"Shit," he said.

He studied Lane's face, saw a quietness overtake her, like a scrim behind her eyes. He recognized that expression—she shut down sometimes, shut people out. She wasn't going to say much else.

"You eat?" he said to Ava.

"No," she said.

"Alright, I'll go pick something up. Give y'all some time."

Oliver left them, drove to the Rouses, and ordered red beans and rice, macaroni and cheese, and fried chicken at the deli counter. He picked up a tray of pecan bars and stood in line. Lane hadn't told him about this visit. Hell, he didn't even know she had a granddaughter.

Things slipped Lane's mind more and more frequently, but mostly they were of little consequence. Something this big—the daughter *died* and she hadn't told him? When had this visit been arranged? He paid for the food and drove back slowly through the neighborhood, taking the long route to avoid the worst potholes. He had a bad feeling about all of this, but he would do what he always did—clean up the mess. He would take care of Lane, whatever she needed.

Chapter 7

Lane rose from her nap to early afternoon light. Her body felt heavy and weak. She needed to fix an iced coffee, smoke, and get back to her research. The restaurant owners wanted their family members depicted in the painting. They'd sent in photos last week that Lane hadn't even glanced at yet. There was so much to do.

What had woken her? Lane had vivid and disturbing dreams. They often left her disoriented, more drained than when she lay down to rest. Lane sighed and stretched, trying to rouse herself. As she shuffled down the long back hall she heard a noise. Perhaps she'd left the radio on? Though it didn't sound like the radio. She listened. A girl's voice.

Lane walked to the sideboard where she kept the pistol, took it out of the drawer. She'd heard about these neighborhood break-ins. Home invasions. The voice was coming from the enclosed porch above the carport. There was nothing in there to steal besides costumes, but she supposed burglars wouldn't know that.

The door was open. It sounded like the girl was on the phone. Is this what they did now, chatted casually with their friends, as if everyone's homes were their personal space. She almost laughed at the absurdity of it. Lane peeked around the doorway. A tall, skinny girl sat cross-legged on the bed. She was pale with dull brown hair, a nothing of a girl.

Lane pointed the gun in her direction and stepped into the room.

"Get out of my house," she said.

The girl stared, her mouth opened in shock.

Lane said, again, "Get out."

The girl seemed frozen, she didn't take her eyes off the gun. Then she smiled, or tried to.

"Lane, you startled me," she said. "Is that real? Is it part of a costume?"

Something was off, it was one of those confusing, dreamlike moments. This girl knew her name. Slowly Lane nodded.

"Yes," she said. "It's part of a costume." Lane tucked the gun in the pocket of her dress, the weight of it making the fabric sag. "I need some caffeine," she said.

The girl followed her to the kitchen. She was tentative. Lane had no patience for these timid, soft types of girls. This was one of those weak ones, Lane could tell. She hovered in the doorway while Lane fixed coffee.

"Is there anything to eat?" Ava asked.

"Look for yourself."

Lane didn't like being near the girl. She took her coffee and went to her studio. She opened her sketchbook and flipped the pages until she found what she hoped was there, an explanation of some sort.

Phone call from Iowa—
Kaitlyn—Louise's friend
Louise is dead
Ava visit June 3

Louise is dead. She read the words and watched her mind skip past them without comprehension. The girl was Ava, then. She checked the date on her phone. Today was the fourth, it added up. Lane reached in her pocket, something heavy tugged at the fabric. She pulled out the gun, turned it over in her hand. She must have meant to clean it. Well. She didn't have time for that now. She put it back in the sideboard.

She remembered the call, this young woman with the broad, flat accent, her daughter's friend. She'd asked the woman how old Ava would be now. Fourteen, Kaitlyn had said.

Lane thought of Louise at fourteen, frown-faced and disapproving. Louise would be thirty-five this year. She'd been away longer than she ever lived here. Time was such a funny creature, the way it coiled, stopped, sped up, reversed. The only measure of it that had relevance to Lane was before, during, after a painting. She could see time in brushstrokes, in line, in an expanse of wall yet to be covered. Time was visual, it spread around doorways, over expanses of plaster.

She turned to a clean page of her sketchbook, blessedly white and absent those three words, *Louise is dead*. She hadn't seen Louise since that Katrina fall, when she'd been working on a hotel ceiling in St. Louis.

She couldn't do those ceiling jobs anymore, on her back all day, on scaffolding. Time was in the body, too. But when Lane was painting, her body disappeared. She forgot to pee, forgot to eat. Forgot everything else. Occasionally she played music, but she forgot to hear it. Even sound fell away. The neighborhood noises and the hum of the refrigerator receded as Lane returned to her drawing.

She was paid top dollar because she put in the effort to get the details right. Her work was sharp and well-executed, and for the last ten years she'd found herself with more job offers than she could take on. Brad Pitt and Angelina Jolie had hired her when they rebuilt their own house after the storm. She did a mural for their dining room.

After that she was featured in *Traditional Home* and *Martha*

81

Stewart and *Southern Living*. She raised her rates and booked more interesting jobs. With the steady work, her painting improved. She was making significant money for the first time, and though she didn't need it—her father had left her plenty, along with the house, plus there was Thomas's life insurance—she felt powerful, accomplished.

But the travel wore on her. Too much anxiety about the details—when the flights left, how long to hold the mail, that sort of thing. She feared her home would be broken into while she was gone. She dreaded the travel itself—missed connections, delays, last-minute gate changes, running in the airport and still missing her plane, having to rebook a new flight and start all over, and C-Span blaring from screens placed every twenty feet. She only worked in town these days. She was getting to be an old woman, she supposed.

She'd been lucky, though, in Katrina. She had a raised house on high ground. The basement took in water, but that's what it was there for. The damage was minimal, and she had been out of town, working in St. Louis. Like a lot of folks, she didn't talk about that year, didn't dwell on it. But New Orleans was different since then. It wasn't the old city she'd always loved. Used to be she knew every one of her neighbors, old families, folks still living where they'd grown up, like Lane.

She brought Oliver in to house-sit while she was away, and kept him on as her assistant after she quit traveling. She was too busy to deal with bills, the arrangements and errands that kept things running smoothly. She was happy to turn that over to someone else, and Oliver was detail-oriented, diligent, funny when he wanted to be. He fetched books from the library for her research, brought in lunches, and remembered to brew cold drip coffee when she was running low. He procured wine and marijuana, dealt with the lawn guy, and helped her keep the parties going.

She'd begun the parties—crawfish boils, live bands in the front room—a year after Thomas died. God, she had energy back then. Raising the girl, painting, keeping up with social obligations. She schmoozed with art people, fought to be included in group shows at galleries, she painted murals at cost to get her work seen, spent more than she made on supplies. Back then everything was a hustle.

The parties were a part of it, too. Reminding folks she was there, inviting important collectors and gallery owners, charming everyone. Her completed canvases prominently displayed above the bar, in the kitchen, throughout the house.

She did the powder room mural on a whim, and people raved about it. To give the small, windowless room a greater sense of space, Lane painted a flawless trompe l'oeil of swamp stretching into the distance, cypresses, shacks on stilts, ibises gleaming white as the porcelain fixtures. Everyone loved it, and she was hired to do private homes by the time Louise was in junior high.

At thirteen Louise had been a pill, constantly criticizing Lane. So Lane wasn't a great mother. Fine. She never claimed to be. Some things were more important than being at every goddamn PTA meeting and volleyball game. Lane was trying, but she had to do everything on her own, and she was busy. At least the girl did well in school, stayed out of trouble. They had their separate lives.

And then she was gone. Run north with some boy. Lane figured it was doomed as all young love and Louise would be back soon enough. With the house to herself Lane found she could relax, could concentrate better. She missed her daughter, worried about her, but everything was easier when she was on her own.

AMO, AMAS, AMAT

JOANNA PEARSON

Not long after they moved into the green Craftsman on the east side of town near us, we began to hear things about the Milandrofers. Mr. Milandrofer was the new Latin teacher at the intermediate school. His wife was from another country—somewhere stark and recently war-ravaged. Everyone had seen Mrs. Milandrofer wandering the grocery store with a dazed expression on her face, pulling brightly colored cereal boxes down to better behold them, only to return them to the shelves again, blinking as if the whole experience was just too much for her.

My mother thought Mrs. Milandrofer was beautiful, and I suppose she did have the sort of thin, extraterrestrial quality one might associate with fashion models. I'd heard Mrs. Milandrofer spoke no English, but when I mentioned this to my mother, she called me rude and asked me how many other languages I spoke. None, I said, which was why I'd signed up for Mr. Milandrofer's

Latin class. "Ah, Latin is wonderful, little rabbit," my mother said, kissing me on the forehead. "You're becoming an intellectual." It was never entirely clear when my mother was mocking me. She had grown up in Tennessee, near a small liberal arts college where her father taught, and from which she'd absorbed many vague notions about the value of intellectualism.

It was my mother, of course, who had gotten me the scholarship that allowed me to attend the private school where Mr. Milandrofer taught. Proper schools, she said, came at a price and provided a classical education. Mr. Milandrofer was a classicist, thus estimable by my mother's measure—although in appearance, he was nothing extraordinary: short, with cheeks the hue and texture of lunch meat, and a gelled frond of dark hair covering his bald patch. Given the disparity in their looks, we assumed that Mrs. Milandrofer, with her long arms and gloomy-gorgeous skeleton face, must have married him only to escape the cold winters and long breadlines of her native land. Maybe he'd gotten her from a bride catalog, my friend Jenny Henderson suggested. At first we were all fond of Mr. Milandrofer, despite the fact that he was nervous and bug-eyed and unlike anyone else in town.

It was from Jenny that I learned the Milandrofers had a child, a little boy named Robert.

"They're weirdos," she told me.

Jenny lived with her mother and stepfather two doors down from us, and she liked to be in the know.

"Mrs. Milandrofer locks herself in her room to cry all day, and the boy has something wrong with him that makes him dumb and fat," Jenny explained, smacking her grape gum authoritatively. "They play opera music really loud, and there's a door no one is allowed to unlock." Jenny was being homeschooled, so she wasn't Mr. Milandrofer's student, but, being a neighbor, she'd been invited over for a cup of tea with her mother shortly after the Milandrofers moved in.

The house was dim, Jenny told me, and filled with small, dainty objects—doilies and ornate lamps with pull chains and porcelain figurines of shepherdesses and little boys playing lutes. Jenny and her mother had had to sit on a stiff, straight-back velveteen couch while Mr. Milandrofer—friendly, anxious, rosy-cheeked—spoke to them and Mrs. Milandrofer brought out tiny plates of dusty cookies and little ceramic cups of tea so weak it tasted like bathwater. Jenny said the boy, Robert, never ventured out to say hello, but she saw him peeking at them from the darkened hallway on occasion, a pale and curious mushroom. When they stood to leave, Jenny's mother inadvertently hit a side table, knocking over a decorative plate depicting a London street scene of red double-decker buses. Mr. Milandrofer responded with a level of distress he could only barely conceal, but even as he reassured Mrs. Henderson that it was no problem, his frantic eyes read otherwise. Indeed, Jenny and her mother could see the dismay in his face as he hastened to usher them out the door before Mrs. Milandrofer returned to the room.

"She never said a word the whole time," Jenny said of Mrs. Milandrofer. "I think she's mute." Mrs. Henderson had wondered why a mother of a young child would have a house full of so many delicate knickknacks in the first place. Such things belonged in the houses of childless couples or prim elderly ladies, she said, not families with children.

We were sitting in Jenny's backyard the afternoon she told me all this. It was not long into the school year, and I had been to Latin class for only a couple of weeks but was already a little taken with Mr. Milandrofer. He certainly wasn't handsome, but there was a look of such gentle concern on his face, such a sense of amused expectation when he spoke to us—"Salvete, discipuli!"—that it stirred me. When I'd turned in my most recent Latin translation, he'd called me to his desk after class, shaking his head as if there were no words sufficient to convey his pleasure.

"What do you want, Margaret?" he'd asked finally, beaming over me, looking beneficent but weary, like someone who has seen great hardships but still retains the capacity for surprise. "What do you want to be someday, a bright girl like you?"

I hadn't quite known how to answer. No one but my mother had taken such an interest in me before. There I was in eighth grade, less grown-up than the other girls, who'd already taken to carrying around little elegantly wrapped tampons in their purses and putting on practiced smirks whenever adults came into their vicinity. My mother worked shifts as a home health aide. She still gave me bowl cuts and dressed me in dungarees, wheat-colored unisex shirts, or puffy sweatpants stained with brown soda that had been handed down from my male cousin. Money was tight, and she viewed me as a child still, an appendage, not a person. Early on, she told me to go to school for as long as I could, collecting degrees like berries on a summer day until I had so many I could overwhelm the world with my knowledge. "No bedpans for you, little rabbit," she said. Her father—in his eighties now, hemiplegic and lodged in a nursing home—had taught English literature at that small college back in Tennessee. Although my mother had been estranged from her father since before I was born, I'd seen a photo of him when he was young: proud and professorial in his tweed vest and glasses, holding his scuffed briefcase.

Now, with Mr. Milandrofer looking expectantly at me, I felt the need to convey to him our common cause.

"I want to be a college professor," I said. "Or a teacher. At a school like this."

He smiled, raising an eyebrow and stepping back, as if to further inspect my intellect.

"Perhaps of Latin?" he said. "You're off to a good start."

"Perhaps," I said, and the word felt good on my tongue, nice and crisp and so much better than plain old maybe. It felt like Mr. Milandrofer and I were already speaking to each other as adults.

"You know," Mr. Milandrofer said, "I could use some assistance. Organizing the textbooks and such. I don't know if you might be willing to help, during lunch, perhaps?"

I felt the tips of my ears going incandescent: so Mr. Milandrofer had surmised my difficulties. He'd passed by me a few days earlier while I was sitting in the arts building hallway, eating my peanut butter sandwich, alone.

To give me a moment to collect myself, he turned and straightened the spine of a volume of Catullus on his shelf. "I don't know," I said, my voice growing hoarse with the threat of tears, the way it did whenever someone was unexpectedly kind.

"If you're too busy, I understand," he said over his shoulder, fiddling with the spines of the Catullus, the Ovid, the *Roma Est Magna*. There were books of Greek poetry, too—hefty and serious-looking. "But I could use the help."

"I'm not all that busy," I said, and Mr. Milandrofer turned back to face me, smiling so broadly that his eyes shrank to two dark commas on his face.

"Wonderful," he said, and he clapped his hands so that the chalk jumped out of its tray behind him.

I forgot myself and smiled full-on at him, allowing my crooked teeth to show. It felt like one of those moments. Like even though he was a middle-aged teacher and I merely his student, something had bloomed, fragile and precious, between us. And even in the end, after all the things people said, long after the Milandrofers had moved away, this was a moment I kept for myself, unsullied.

My mother was my best friend during those years. This is always a dangerous and questionable thing to say, but it was true. Jenny Henderson was the only friend I had who was my own age. Our mothers worked together, and after school I would go to Jenny's house, where we'd wait for them to finish their shifts.

"Omnia Gallia in tres partes divisa est," I said for Jenny's benefit. She was smarter, so sometimes I liked to lord over her the things I picked up in class. We lay on our backs in Jenny's backyard, flicking acorns over a fence and studying the sky. One lazy, anvil-shaped cloud drifted overhead. I looked to see if Jenny seemed impressed. She possessed the motley knowledge of an autodidact with a library card and an instinct for mischief. Her mom worked as much as mine did, so her homeschooling amounted to Jenny marauding the interlibrary loan system, watching PBS, and wandering feral through the neighborhood. There'd been some behavior issues back in her old parochial school, my mother said—I understood this to mean Jenny had been kicked out—and the public schools were too dangerous. Full of knives and oxy and pregnant teenagers.

"Show-off," Jenny said. "Latin is bullshit."

Instead of flicking the acorn over the fence, I flicked it toward her face. She gave me a shove. Jenny was scrappy and brave, untroubled by anyone else's opinion, nothing like the other girls at my school.

"Latin is the language of law, science, and logic," I recited.

She laughed.

"Come on. Let's look for dildos."

Jenny stood, brushing leaves off her shorts, and I rose to follow. She was obsessed with contraband, most recently dildos. She'd found one once, abandoned in the wooded gully behind the houses. There was a patch of scraggly woods behind Jenny's neighborhood that abutted an abandoned housing development called Nottingham Bend. These half-built Nottingham houses stared out, impassive, through the trees. Often Jenny and I scrabbled down the embankment, wandering through the adjoining woods. Hobos lived here, Jenny told me, and she could sometimes hear their hobo sex cries at night.

"You're a pervert," I told her.

When Jenny first showed me the dildo—big as a man's fist, florid and rubbery, with hyperreal veins—I felt nauseated.

"You're just not used to men," Jenny said, her voice going rich and delicious with secrets, the voice she used whenever she had special knowledge to impart. "Men have certain needs. There are things they have to do."

In addition to her stepfather, Karl, Jenny lived with an older stepbrother, Todd, who was a student at the community college and who, people said, sold pills. Todd and Karl were a mostly invisible presence in the household whenever I was there, but, like wild animals, they left traces of themselves—stained socks, athletic shorts, muddy work boots, half-eaten bags of corn chips—like scat along a forest trail.

It was true I wasn't used to men. Their proximity elicited a jangly alertness in me. There had been times I'd felt Todd's and Karl's eyes on us—not me, really, but my mother, who was, by all accounts, still beautiful. She'd had me at eighteen, derailing a promising academic career. My mother had been a debate champion, brilliant in every way, a full scholarship to a fancy university awaiting her, until my arrival threw things off.

Jenny rolled her eyes whenever I spoke of my mother with admiration. But I couldn't help myself. My mother still carried herself with a certain pride, wearing red lipstick to work and toting around a copy of a Dostoyevsky to read during lulls. Compared with her, all the other mothers I knew looked rumpled and over-stuffed, like badly-slept-upon pillows. Jenny insisted my mother was a snob, her small efforts acts of pretension.

"Come on," she said.

We picked our way through the bushes behind Jenny's house, down through the dead honeysuckle branches and pine straw. We'd lost the original dildo. Jenny had known better than to take it home, so we had buried it under leaves by a large oak down at the bottom of the gully. A hobo must have reclaimed it, Jenny decided.

A bird called, rising with a flap from the branches above us. The bare beams of the half-built houses in Nottingham Bend loomed over the next crest. No one knew if these houses would ever be finished now that the Anheuser plant had left town. Jenny hoped Nottingham Bend would remain abandoned. She wanted to meet these so-called hobos. The way she described them, they were a merry band of misfits whiling away their days with gaudy dildos and dog-eared *National Geographics*, family-size bags of Doritos, and old paperbacks and cans of Milwaukee's Best. I imagined them, swearing and tattooed, full of banter, manning the sterns of the empty houses like jolly pirates.

To Jenny, the gully between her neighborhood and Nottingham Bend was a prospector's paradise. We had found all sorts of human flotsam and jetsam down there—ratty army blankets, a ziplock bag full of old Canadian pennies, and, once, a whole, perfect birthday cake iced with the words HAPPY BIRTH-DAY, MIKE! Jenny swore she'd met someone there once: a skinny man in a fisherman's vest who'd been smoking a pipe and reading a copy of *On the Road*. He'd talked to Jenny about his life philosophy and hopping railroad cars, she said—details so generic they left me almost certain she'd made the whole thing up.

"I found a shopping cart the other day," she said now. "And an old green refrigerator with a bottle of gin in it. I'll show you."

I followed her, picking my way over the large stones that were strewn along the gully like irregular steps. A trickle of dirty water flowed beneath our feet. Over to our left, a lone squirrel snuffled in the leaves, inspecting an abandoned red Solo cup. When we were younger, Jenny and I had pretended this was a great canyon. We'd hopped from stone to stone, talking of wizardry and elves. Now we hunted for dildos, pages torn out of old girlie magazines, interesting hunks of machinery, train-hopping strangers.

There was a rustle of leaves around the bend. Jenny hissed,

pinching the flesh of my arm to stop me from talking. I froze. In truth, I was terrified of stumbling upon one of Jenny's hobos.

We stood there for a second, but now the only noise was from a distant lawnmower. Then the rustling started again, like the sound of a small animal burrowing into its nest.

Jenny gestured for me to follow.

A little boy, maybe five or six, was sitting on his haunches in the leaves. When he heard us, he looked up, and I saw that his face was smeared dark, like that of a predator feasting after a kill. He clutched a partially gnawed chocolate bar, big as a cutting board, the kind you might give as a novelty gift.

"Robert?" Jenny called out, and the boy shot us a look of guilt and terror and clutched the chocolate bar closer to his chest.

"It's okay," I said, realizing now that this must be the Milandrofers' little boy. Just as Jenny had said, there was something vacant about his eyes. Instinctively, I tried to make my voice soothing. "Did you get lost? Can we take you home?"

Robert nodded, docile, dutifully wrapping the chocolate back in its foil. As we scrambled up the embankment, he allowed Jenny to hold his hand.

I followed the two of them to the green house. At the door we knocked and knocked again, but there was no answer. Finally, Robert simply opened the door and we all went inside.

"Where's your mother?" Jenny asked.

The house was quiet except for the ticking of a clock in the hallway, and, as Jenny had said, it was dark. The walls were cluttered with decoration: framed images of angels perched on puffy clouds, a poster of Monet's *Water Lilies*, a black-and-white movie still of Humphrey Bogart and Lauren Bacall, a framed copy of the Lord's Prayer in looping cursive script. There were no family photos, no school photos of Robert. The living room was so crammed with objects that it looked like a junk shop. An old radio stood in one corner next to a coatrack made to look like a pear tree. A collection of commemorative thimbles hung in a little glass case above a peach-colored settee. I picked up a music box with a dancing bear atop it and traced a line through the film of dust.

A door opened. I heard the clatter of keys in the kitchen, followed by the sound of footsteps.

We turned to find Mr. Milandrofer standing in front of us. Robert ran to him, throwing his chubby little arms around his father's waist, smashing his chocolatey face right into Mr. Milandrofer's pants.

"Jenny? Margaret?"

A shadow fell over his face like a curtain over a window.

"We found him," Jenny said, pointing to Robert. "In the woods."

Mr. Milandrofer's expression remained inscrutable. He was still wearing the pale blue shirt I'd seen him teach in earlier, but it looked rumpled now, yellowish stains under his arms.

"Where's Mama?" he asked Robert.

Robert pointed one grubby finger to the ceiling. "Sleeping," he said.

"Thank you, girls," Mr. Milandrofer said, then ushered us toward the door. "Mrs. Milandrofer gets bad headaches sometimes."

Once we were outside, he handed us two lollipops from his pocket, as if we were good children getting a treat from a bank teller.

We licked our lollipops all the way back to Jenny's house, where we found my mom and Jenny's stepbrother, Todd, drinking glasses of Coca-Cola in the kitchen.

"Where were you?" my mother asked, and her cheeks were bright, like she'd been laughing hard. Her eyes shone in that way they did when she was receiving a particular type of attention. Todd turned on the tap and filled another glass with water, taking a gulp.

"Your mom's not home yet, kid," he said to Jenny.

"We found the neighbor boy," she announced. "He was lost in the woods and we rescued him."

My mother's eyes still shone with a feverish light, but her cheeks were returning to their normal color. "Well, aren't you two girls just brilliant things," she said, her words light as confetti. "Wouldn't you say so, Todd?"

Todd grunted his assent, but I saw something in his face: the way his eyes followed my mother as if awaiting her approval, the way he touched her wrist quickly, communicating something not meant for the rest of us to see. It was all over in a matter of seconds. Jenny did a performative little twirl, but it was my mother, standing there in the late sunlight streaming through the kitchen window, who looked shining and divine, like someone out of Mr. Milandrofer's poetry. Her wine-dark lips parted and she laughed, clutching her white arms, my radiant, god-born mother. Jenny tugged my sleeve, but I ignored her like she was nothing but a housefly brushing against my elbow.

When my mother heard I was helping Mr. Milandrofer at lunchtime, she was pleased.

"You learn your Latin, little rabbit," my mother said. "You know, my daddy read Latin and Greek. He was fluent in Italian, French, and Spanish, with passable German, too."

I coughed and said nothing. It was hard for me to understand how she could speak so proudly of her father. And yet I'd learned better than to say anything bad about him in front of her.

From her crossword puzzle—she liked to do them whenever she had the time, "to keep the mind agile," she'd told me—my mother looked up at me and took the capped end of her pen between her teeth. Talking about her father always made her go soft-eyed and sad.

"Never forget yourself because of a man," she said, dropping the pen and letting her gaze drift to something invisible on the horizon.

I understood that my mother meant my own father. I knew little of him other than that he'd been a graduate student of my grandfather's. Older. Married. He'd left when my mother was eight months pregnant with me. My father's departure—and my arrival—had been the reason why she moved away.

Ever since then, my mother had tempered any attraction she felt toward men with a hard suspicion. She probably would have been wary of Mr. Milandrofer had she not yet met him. She didn't say so, but I could tell by the way she'd nodded after giving him the once-over that he was suitably unsexed by his double chin and doughy features, the bad mustache he wore, his poorly tucked shirts. He was simply a teacher. Harmless.

Besides, everyone knew Mr. Milandrofer was pining for his wife. People spoke of this: how she'd married him only for the green card, and how poor, smitten Mr. Milandrofer was now desperate to win her love. You just had to look at all the little gifts with which he'd plied her to see. "He's besotted," the owner of the local deli said after Mr. Milandrofer called again and again to special-order a particular type of sausage, something that Mrs. Milandrofer had loved in her childhood. When people saw them together in public, they noticed Mr. Milandrofer's solicitousness, how anxious and attentive he seemed.

"Go study your Latin," my mother said, waving a hand at me. "Make Mr. Milandrofer proud."

After that, Mr. Milandrofer didn't mention the time I'd dropped Robert off at his house. We spent most of our time at school together quietly. I'd grown accustomed to this: the comfortable silence of our shared lunch breaks punctuated every now and then by an observation on a particular passage from one of the Latin texts or a tricky declension. Mr. Milandrofer let me pore through his books while the radiator hummed and rattled behind us.

"You know," he said one day, "if there are things you ever want to talk about—" He paused, removing his glasses and rubbing his watery eyes. He was eating tuna salad, and he placed the fork down on his desk thoughtfully. "I want to be a trusted adult. Someone you can ask questions. About worries. Or feelings."

I felt a dark, muddy warmth blossoming at my chest and spreading upward.

"What feelings?" I said.

"I ran into your friend Jenny Henderson again," he said, looking out the window, as if he were changing the subject. "She's a nice girl. A spitfire."

I nodded.

"You two seem quite close."

"She's basically my only other friend," I said—and immediately blushed at my choice of words. Yet if Mr. Milandrofer picked up on the implication, he didn't show it.

"Adolescence is an overwhelming time," he said. "Just promise me you'll come talk to me if you're feeling confused. Or if you're feeling alone."

"I will," I said.

"Thank you, pious Aeneas," Mr. Milandrofer said, and he snapped the plastic lid onto his empty lunch container. The room smelled of tuna, but I was accustomed to this. The food Mr. Milandrofer brought to eat was always hearty and disgusting— mayonnaisey raisin-pocked salads, bachelor food, meals I knew no loving wife would ever pack. Certainly I wouldn't have packed them for Mr. Milandrofer.

He got up, walked over to me, and gave me two pats on the head. When he called me "pious Aeneas," I knew he was pleased with me. The book open on my desk showed an illustration of two young Roman men in togas who appeared to be wrestling each other. Mr. Milandrofer's hand fell over it, his fingers tracing the contours of the sketch. Right then we were reading bits of Vergil in translation in class, then trying them in the original. To inspire us, he'd said. Advanced work, a challenge. The other students grumbled. The funny kids called Aeneas *Anus* and Dido *Dildo*, and the class laughed like this was a big hoot. They preferred the days when we draped sheets around ourselves as togas, celebrating Saturnalia and discussing Roman culture. Once, when handsome Justin Giddings, a lacrosse star whose parents were both attorneys, stood in his chair, shouting "Veni, vidi, vici" in falsetto and sashaying his hips, I'd watched Mr. Milandrofer smile patiently, although I could swear I heard him curse under his breath.

"You and I, we are a team, aren't we, discipula?" he said to me that day during lunch. It was a thing he'd said before, but he said it that day with extra emphasis, like we were fellow Trojans battling a sea of Justin Giddingses, who loped around the school with all the infuriating grace and indolence of young laureates.

Jenny had been colder to me in recent weeks, more aloof. I was used to this: her moods, the way she lit up from within with pleasure or irritation. When I arrived after school, the doors to her house would be locked and she would be nowhere to be found. I would search the neighborhood, wandering and calling until I found her: in a neighbor's backyard hammock, or inside one of the abandoned houses at Nottingham Bend, her eyes glowing like a wild creature's from the dark.

That particular day, the door to Jenny's house was locked. Jenny had always loved being outside, but we'd also spend time in her house—watching TV or eating popcorn while we listened to music in her bedroom. Now she was never there. She only wanted to be outside.

I found Jenny sitting in the base of a hollowed tree down in the gully.

"Hey," I said.

She didn't look up at me. I saw she'd been drinking one of the fruity wine coolers her mother kept in the refrigerator. Her mouth was stained pinkish, like that of a child with a glass of Kool-Aid in summer.

"You were hiding from me." She took a swig.

"Want to play Truth or Dare?" Jenny asked.

I sat down beside her.

"It's not that fun with just us."

"Sure it is. Choose."

I knew better than to allow Jenny to dare me.

"Truth."

"Who do you *like?*" she asked, putting emphasis on the last word, tossing the empty bottle of wine cooler across the gully, where it landed with a soft thud in the brush. She didn't meet my eye.

I thought of Mr. Milandrofer, his sweet, dorky smile and mustache, the way he smelled of coffee even in the afternoon, the way his voice rose in enthusiasm, his mustache lifting when he smiled, revealing his small, perfect teeth. I cleared my throat.

"Justin Giddings, I guess," I said.

Jenny snorted. "Justin Giddings is an idiot," she said, yet something had broken open in her voice again, sun parting clouds, and I knew she was not unhappy with my answer. We were still friends. She touched me lightly on the back of my neck, and I shivered. "You're a fool," she said. "A silly little fool."

"Who do *you* like?" I asked, mock-angrily.

"I don't choose truth," Jenny said, her expression gone sly. "I choose dare."

"I dare us to go to your house and watch TV."

"Dare me to go to the Milandrofers' house," she said, her voice airy and reckless. "Dare me to sneak into their creepy old house and see what those weirdos do when no one else is around."

"I don't dare you to do that."

"Dare me to go find your *boyfriend*, Mr. Milandrofer," Jenny said, her voice singsongy, sickly sweet like cough syrup.

"No. That's not the dare."

But Jenny was already off, tearing through the leaves, scrambling up the opposite hillside.

"Wait," I shouted. "Jenny."

She turned, laughing over her shoulder once more, then disappeared above the crest of the hill. I went after her, knowing the dare was already in action.

There was nothing to do but follow her into their house.

I entered from the backyard through the patio door. Inside, the Milandrofers' house was quiet and dark and still. I moved through the kitchen, where plates were piled high in the sink. An opened can of tomato soup sat on the counter next to a half-empty sleeve of store-bought chocolate chip cookies.

"Jenny?" I whispered, tiptoeing through the hallways and into the living room, which was even more stuffed and haphazard than I remembered.

"Jenny?"

Someone padded down the stairs and into the living room, and I started. It wasn't Jenny. It was Robert.

He peered at me from behind a chair, holding a ratty blanket in one hand and an orange Popsicle in the other.

"Hi, Robert," I whispered, kneeling down and making my face friendly.

Robert took a long, slow slurp of his ice pop and then, removing it, stuck out his orange tongue. It wasn't a rude gesture. He smiled a sticky orange smile and looked up at me.

"Have you seen my friend? Jenny?" I gestured to the darkened hallway beyond the living room.

He gazed at me, unblinking, sucking on his lower lip. I was beginning to wonder if he even understood. Then he turned from me, moseying through the living room dreamily, lifting up his mother's miniature ballet dancer, her tiny bejeweled elephant, for inspection. Then, at the doorway, he paused, as if waiting for me to follow.

I did, creeping after him as he went up the staircase, appalled at Jenny's audacity. We made our way down a long hallway, passing several closed doors until we reached the one at the very end of the hall. Robert opened it, and I saw another set of unfinished stairs.

"She's up there?" I asked.

Robert just looked at me, long and slow. He took another lick of his Popsicle, then began climbing.

I followed him into a large, unfinished attic with a pitched ceiling and a planked floor. The room looked like a nursery in a storybook orphanage. It was filled with white bassinets and cradles, a dozen at least, arranged in neat rows under the eaves. In a rocking chair, Mrs. Milandrofer sat holding a lifelike baby doll in her arms. She wore a green silk robe with fuzzy slippers and had drawn two high, arching lines above her actual eyebrows, which had been plucked to nothing. She looked like a washed-up old movie star, someone marked by glamour and tragedy.

Robert ran to her, grabbing the green tail of her robe, and she rose from the rocker, putting the baby down with a shushing sound. I stood immobilized at the top of the steps, hidden behind a large chest of drawers. I had the sense I'd barged in upon a moment of private, personal necessity, like accidentally walking into an occupied restroom stall.

"Babies," Robert said flatly.

"Babies," Mrs. Milandrofer echoed. Her voice was high-pitched and strange, the voice of someone who did not speak often. She picked up another baby doll, patting its bottom soothingly and whispering consolations into its ear, before replacing it gently in its cradle. She murmured a strange word, once, and then again, and I understood this must be the baby's name.

She moved to a tiny white cupboard painted with pink rosettes and opened it gently. Inside were little bottles and rattles and blankets. She selected a bottle and a blanket for one of the baby dolls near the dormer window. I watched her move through the room, lifting each plastic doll lovingly from its bassinet, cooing and adjusting blankets. Robert followed her, dull-eyed in his red sweatpants, sucking at some orange goo on his finger.

She spoke in such a low tone to the dolls in their bassinets that I couldn't make out her words. I guessed she was speaking in another language, something harsh yet lilting that made me imagine rolling green hills and rushing waters—somewhere far from here, with actual wilderness instead of gullies filled with trash behind abandoned subdivisions.

Mrs. Milandrofer knelt toward one of the bassinets and scooped up a baby doll. Holding it against her shoulder, she patted its back gently. "Shh, shh," she whispered, before putting it back down.

Robert followed her, murmuring to himself. He tugged at her arm. When she did not respond, he pulled up his blue shirt, exposing his belly, smooth and white and fat as a moon, and started jumping up and down. He sucked at the hem of his shirt, making a sound like *glob-glob-glob*.

Mrs. Milandrofer sighed. Turning off the attic light switch, she took Robert's hand. I pressed myself back against the wall, further behind the dresser, to hide myself as they passed me on their way back down the stairs. Mrs. Milandrofer closed the attic door behind her, and I let out a breath. I was alone—except for all of Mrs. Milandrofer's babies.

I looked into one of the nearby cradles. A baby doll stared up at me, one plastic eye open, a cracked seam running down the front of its face like a scar. I picked up the doll and it rested, hollow and light in my arms. A bead of sweat rolled from one of my armpits down my side. The attic was hot, the air musty, and my throat had gone dry.

I moved quietly down the stairs back to the attic door, but

when I tried to open it, I found it could only be opened from the outside. There was no inside handle. I pushed at the door, beat on it with my hands. Panicking, I called to Robert, to Mrs. Milandrofer, to anyone, but there was no answer.

I walked back up the attic stairs. Looking out the little dormer window, I saw Mrs. Milandrofer and Robert outside. It was starting to rain. She wore a black raincoat and a pert little hat. Robert had on a jacket printed with yellow ducks. From the attic window, they looked unreal, like tiny mechanical figures. The window wouldn't open; no one would be able to hear me from outside.

Even though the attic was stuffy and warm, a chill fell over me. All was very still.

For a long time I sat there, with all of Mrs. Milandrofer's precious babies surrounding me, silent in their swaddling, while the sun dropped and the attic light grew thinner and thinner, until finally I saw Mr. Milandrofer's car pull into the drive. Then I ran down the steps to beat upon the attic door again, kicking and shouting again, my voice growing hoarse, until Mr. Milandrofer either heard or sensed something was wrong. It was he who finally opened the door.

"Margaret?" he asked. "What in the world are you doing here?"

I was starting to answer when I saw Mrs. Milandrofer standing behind him, uttering words I could not understand.

"I'm sorry," I said, not even attempting any real explanation. "I got stuck."

Something whirled past my head and hit the wall beside me. I turned to look and saw a little pewter dish lying on the floor.

"You should leave," Mr. Milandrofer said. Behind him rose a great, animal wail.

The next day, I could barely bring myself to look at Mr. Milandrofer during Latin class. I could feel the weight of his avoidance, the note of contrition in his voice when he turned in my direction, not once meeting my gaze, and didn't go to his classroom at lunchtime—not that day, or ever again.

Mr. Milandrofer eventually took another student under his wing: a friendless boy named James Jankowicz who rarely spoke but who turned in flawless work in all his classes. James began studying Greek, I heard. Once, passing through the hallways during the lunch hour, I saw him sitting at a desk with a book open in front of him. Over him, Mr. Milandrofer bent forward, gesticulating.

One afternoon I found Jenny at our old spot in the woods after school.

She was sitting on a stump at the base of the embankment, smoking a cigarette inexpertly.

"Watch this," she said, attempting to blow a ring of smoke and coughing.

"Cool," I said, crouching on the damp leaves next to her.

She took another drag and turned to me, her eyes narrow and adult.

"I didn't really go into their house the other day," she said.

"I know," I said. "I went there to look for you."

I told her about Mrs. Milandrofer and the attic and all the dolls, the long hours I'd spent trapped among them.

Her eyes widened. After I finished talking, she stood up.

"Come here," she said. "There's something you should see."

I followed her again along the stones that lay in the trickle of dirty water there at the bottom of the gully. We picked our way a long while, following the stream until we finally reached a point where I could hear the rumble of an overpass above us, just ahead. We were farther out than we'd ever walked, long past Jenny's neighborhood or Nottingham Bend.

A large forked tree leaned from one bank over the other, like a suspended drawbridge. Jenny helped me across it.

"Look."

All along the gully were the dismembered bodies of baby dolls. It looked like a toy store massacre. Blond or brunette or bald, the heads lay toppled among the leaves. Some were wide-eyed; some appeared to be peacefully sleeping. Elsewhere the bodies lay splayed, chunky arms extended in feeble protest, tiny fists or tiny hands reaching into empty air.

I swallowed.

Jenny picked up a decapitated baby doll head and studied it for a long moment. Then, turning to me, she tossed the doll head like a baseball so that it arced into the brush ahead of us.

"None of this was here before," she said.

"People," I said, exhaling like I was about to say something profound.

Jenny nodded like she was agreeing with me. "People are fucking frauds," she said.

"That's not what I meant."

She rolled her eyes and tipped her head back. "Oh, Margaret. You're so oblivious."

"No, I'm not."

"You know why your mom is always over at our house?" she said. "I mean, half the time, my mom's not even there." She looked at me, hard, as if she were inspecting me for something.

I had no answer. The babies in the forest gazed skyward, each lost in its private contemplations. I thought of my mother, her slash of bright lipstick and her books, the way she moved through the world, proud, queenly. I could imagine her standing above the blaze of funeral pyres, like Dido, deified by her people. Or perhaps just a fool, leaping pointlessly into a fire. Love made you foolish. This was a thing my mother often said—she'd learned. She knew better.

"I've heard them," Jenny said. She was no longer looking at me now, and her voice sounded tired. "It's why I try to stay away." She sighed, kicking the chubby foot of a baby to the side. "You know, Margaret, you're so stupid. Like a little kid."

I didn't answer her, but I felt very old then, almost ancient, older than the rocks or the soil or the largest trees that hung over us.

We stood in silence, gazing at the babies for what felt like a long time.

Before the school year ended, new rumors started about Mr. Milandrofer, that he'd been spotted roaming the half-finished houses of Nottingham Bend at odd hours. It was a meetup spot, people said—you know, for *that* type.

People said other things, too. For instance, that Magdalena Milandrofer had lodged a domestic assault charge against her husband, although many people claimed it was actually she who had assaulted him. There was something fierce about Magdalena Milandrofer, everyone said. She seemed like a person you wouldn't want to cross. Just before the final weeks of school, Mr. Milandrofer resigned from his job. We heard the Milandrofers would be moving out before the month ended.

Jenny and I stood a few paces back from their house, watching as movers hauled the ottoman and grandfather clock and box after box of Mrs. Milandrofer's belongings into a large moving truck. I thought of Robert, sucking at the fat slug of his fist, and of Mrs. Milandrofer, lost in her caretaking of all those baby dolls, and of Mr. Milandrofer, his eager greetings and the palpable edges of his loneliness. I could almost imagine him picking his way through the scraggly branches and stray dildos and broken babies to the graffitied, half-built walls of Nottingham Bend, where he'd be met by shadowy faces, shadowy hands, and a certain type of solace.

Once my mother had told me of a time not long after I was born when she was alone and uncertain, a disgraced teenager with an infant, kicked out of her parents' house, driving away from the only place she'd ever known. Banished. "You wouldn't stop crying," she told me, "but the more you cried, the lonelier I felt."

I asked her what she did then, thinking she might say she pulled over to comfort me and was, in turn, comforted. I could picture it, the two of us a single, fused shape. Then a moment of revelation: my mother would be moved from her desolation by a sign—a hawk streaking across the sky, a liquid orange-pink sunrise, or a kindly old woman appearing like an angel to offer her a cup of truck-stop coffee—something that suggested that we are all being watched and cared for in our worst moments, that an omnipotent hand might on occasion reach down from the storm-tossed sky.

My mother did not answer me at first. "I kept driving," she said. "I kept driving, and eventually you calmed yourself and stopped."

THE SINGING MEMBRANE

F.E. CHOE

The glassblower is unsettled by the number of migratory birds accumulating on the roof of her cottage. Leggy blue-white herons, arctic terns, exhausted city street pigeons. They sun uninvited on the roof, tip over dead potted plants to avail themselves of dust baths, strip the paint from her car with their droppings.

Each day more arrive. Barn owls, chaffinches, crows. A parakeet with clipped wings that has traveled unharmed in the claws of a condor. It tumbles softly into the dirt of the front garden bed when released, shakes itself off, hops close enough that the glassblower can read the neon green band on its leg. The brittle strip, like the discarded ring from a plastic bottle cap, bears the name of a beach town fifteen-hundred miles to the south.

Once upon a time, the glassblower lived an ordinary life in a tiny house in an unremarkable neighborhood. She had a husband, a daughter, and the sort of predictable existence people find reassuring. A mothering garden with marrow that sent up long blooms like silk purses in summer, peppers that stung the tips of her fingers when plucked from the stem.

There were reliable weekly Sunday dinners with in-laws, a bedtime routine. The glassblower and her husband would put their baby to bed at eight p.m., and when the baby woke at one a.m., the glassblower would go to her, lift her out of her crib, sing (badly, though the baby never seemed to mind) and rock her back to sleep. When the baby inevitably woke again at four a.m. then it was the glassblower's husband's turn to go soothe her, and she would listen for his voice through the wall calling them all to sleep, *sleep, baby, sleep.*

One morning, two cranes greet the glassblower in the kitchen. On the floor between them is the gold wrapper from the last of her butter, the foil picked clean.

She makes no remark about the disappeared butter, the fridge door left ajar, the mess of droppings they have left on her cottage floor. She only reaches into a cabinet for her last bag of rice, scatters a handful on the ground, watches them bow their red crowns and eat.

The glassblower says nothing. Her mother taught her nothing—to be nothing if not hospitable to guests.

The birds multiply rapidly after that. They steal into windows and pull apart her mattress for their nests. The glassblower finds eggs in the eaves of the cottage, nestled in with her underwear and t-shirts in the dresser drawers. She layers pile after pile of wood shavings across the floorboards of the cottage, surrenders her bedroom and pads the sagging couch with an old quilt, picks feathers from her sleeves and hair each morning when she wakes.

At night the rafters creak and moan under the weight of their bodies. The glassblower is terrified the roof will cave in. She tries not to think of this too much.

The glassblower tries not to think of a lot of things.

What her ex-husband might be doing at that very moment in their two-bedroom home in its unremarkable neighborhood while she shivers under a shitty blanket in the middle of nowhere.

Who her ex-husband might be fucking. If her ex-husband wakes up at four in the morning for no reason at all anymore.

She thinks of the glass animals she used to make in her studio in the city. Sets of multicolored, striated fish that she would line up along the shop window to catch the light. She recalls a calliope hummingbird that took her five months to make, its throat jeweled with drops of crimson like pomegranate seeds. She thinks of firing animal after animal in the furnace. Bees, dragonflies, jellyfish, doves.

She thinks of how you shape a bullfrog gullet first, how its singing membrane swells with life at the end of the blowpipe. How your breath expands and stretches its walls of rounded glass as it cools and hardens to hold shape.

The baby's name was Ava.

The glassblower says it over and over in the close dark. She says it as she stands over the iron stove and watches the water come to a boil. She says it as she chops wood and lets the axe handle bite callouses into the skin of her palms.

An invocation. Confession, penance.

Ava. Ava. Ava. Ava.

Sometimes the glassblower thinks of tethering the birds to the roof. How she will have to cut the ivy away from the foundation so the vines will not fasten them to the ground.

She thinks of the kick and tug of a sudden separation from the earth, splinters of sky seen through the cracks in the floorboards. She thinks of the sound a cottage makes when lifted by thousands of wings.

Wild, insatiable, like a small sudden thunderstorm. Like the sky is as real and tender as skin, solid enough to beat wings against, to cut into, to slip behind.

DOGWOOD

YURINA YOSHIKAWA

"Wake up."

I was just in our old kitchenette waiting for the red kettle to boil.

"Daddy."

The room is dark and I can hardly see anything. I was just in the middle of a dream that was also a memory.

"Wake up," he repeats in whispers even though I'm already up. "Daddy wake up wake up wake up."

Both of his hands are on the duvet I'm rolled up in, rocking me side to side. His hands feel more like little paws, urgent yet weak.

It's been a couple of weeks since we moved in, and I still have trouble remembering where I am in moments like these. I fish around the side table for my glasses and take Max's cheeks into my palms. From the moisture I can tell that he's been crying.

"What's the matter, bud?"

"You didn't wake up."

"I'm up now."

"But not when I wanted you to."

I tap my phone to check the time: 2:16 a.m. I have notifications for 18 new messages that I swipe away. I motion for Max to come snuggle with me in bed.

"Your arms feel cold," I say.

My eyes have adjusted to the dark and I can see his head shaking. "I want you to come to my room. I want..." His voice turns into mumbles.

"You want what? I couldn't really hear."

"Just...come. There's a monster in my room."

I can't help sighing—it's already out. I try to course-correct and pat his silky hair. "Monsters aren't real. Remember?"

"I know, but... You said once that grown-ups can be wrong sometimes. So maybe you're wrong."

I did say that, but I didn't expect him to remember it so well. I hardly remember that day myself, when we cremated his mother and he asked me why she had died when she did, even though the doctors thought she would live for many more years. I said something about how there's still a lot we don't know about the human body, that sometimes doctors didn't even know why things happened the way they did. We all thought the treatment was going well.

I remember saying something like, *Things happen that we can't explain. Sometimes, we think one thing, and we find out later that we were wrong.*

I can feel him trembling so I agree to come take a look, but on the condition that after I get rid of the monster, we'll come back to my queen-size bed and sleep here together.

He whispers, "Deal," and holds out one hand for the "formal shake," as he calls it.

I shake his hand like I do with adults. "It's gonna be okay," I say. "Everything's gonna be okay." Even in the fog of sleep deprivation, I know how useless and unhelpful I sound. Naoko would have been able to say it in a way that actually willed everything to be okay. We slowly make our way to the hallway.

Max hesitates to enter his own room and points to the window. "There."

"That's where you saw it?"

He nods.

As we get closer, I can see the outlines of the tall trees out the window and the vast backyard that seems to have no end. It's windy tonight and the wind is rustling.

"Hmm," I say. "Good news—I don't see any monsters here."

Max shakes his head in protest.

"I spy something red—"

"I don't want to play I Spy. I want to go home."

"This is our home."

"No, Daddy, I don't like it here. How long do we have to stay here anyway?"

I crouch down and hug him, partly to comfort him, but mostly so I can avoid looking at his face. I've dreaded this moment when I would be confronted with this question of whether or not I made the right decision, moving the two of us all the way here from New York, where I had lived for the last fifteen years, and Max had spent his whole life of six and a half years. We lived in a tiny prewar one-bedroom apartment in Brooklyn, barely 900 square feet, and this house in Dogwood, Tennessee, is about three times as spacious but probably just as old. There are still boxes everywhere, some half-opened, others not opened at all. I prioritized getting Max's room ready first, thinking he would be more excited about our new life here the sooner he felt at home. The walls are still bare, but his clothes are in drawers. The "I Can Read" books are stacked on shelves, and his beloved Legos are either still in their containers or scattered on the floor as little spaceships.

Max sniffles into my shirt.

"It's okay," I whisper. "We'll get more used to it over time. We'll go get a night light tomorrow. And a curtain. Maybe we'll check out a home goods store or something. See more of the town. Yeah?"

"This place gives me the creeps," Max says. "What if the monster comes back?"

I scan the titles on his bookshelf. "Maybe I can read something to you?" I glimpse the spine of *Goodnight, Moon* on the bookshelf and quickly look away. I had tossed or donated more than half of our belongings in New York, but one of the few books we kept is this copy of *Goodnight, Moon*. He's clearly aged out of it, but this version has a button that plays a recording of Naoko's voice reading the words. Even in the darkness, and even just from the spine, the stark color schemes of orange, green, and yellow stand out. The tree branches are now tapping the glass every few seconds from the wind.

"Or we can go back to my room," I say. "I'll whisper a story in your ear."

We slowly make our way back to where we started. Finally, like I had suggested in the first place, we snuggle together under the big white duvet, where I whisper-sing him the lyrics to "Puff, the Magic Dragon" because I realize I can't come up with a story on my own, and I figure this song has a narrative arc, albeit a tragic one. After the first few verses I can feel his body heating up. His eyelids are closed. As exhausted as I am, I need something to help me fall back asleep, so I carefully roll over to the other side, find my phone, and watch videos of late-night comedians on mute with captions.

As I watch and scroll, I'm reminded of what these nighttime hours had felt like over the last few years. Being here in Dogwood, doing this now, I can fool my brain into thinking she's not really gone, we're just separated due to work. As a wildlife documentary filmmaker, I've been called away to different cities throughout America, sometimes Canada or South America, and it wasn't unusual for me to not see Naoko and Max for months at a time. Naoko worked, too, as a freelance producer for indie documentaries that were human-focused, as she liked to say, in stark contrast to my work. Her projects took longer, sometimes years, but each film of hers was a work of art, whereas my projects were commissioned by corporate networks to be seen by the dwindling audience of cable TV. If we were lucky, a one-minute clip that we took of an armadillo might get a million views because of some arbitrary meme. But we believed in our work, and rooted for each other, and took turns with the household whenever one of us had downtime. It's hard for me to admit even now, but circumstantially, and financially, this meant Naoko was home more often than me, and I had constantly felt like I had to catch up to parenthood every time I was back at home with Max.

In the current video clip I'm watching, a comedian is doing a bit about being stuck in an elevator with another person who thinks they can solve it by pressing all the buttons.

Naoko and I had met in grad school for filmmaking, and we had so many dreams in the beginning of making something together. She would write the story and I would direct it. We even made a bulletin board of notes and images that inspired us, but after we became a family, the lists of ideas turned into grocery lists, and cut-outs from film mags were replaced by printouts from sonograms and eventually, Max's growth.

At the funeral, there were so many people there, from her family, coworkers, college friends, childhood friends, so many faces I didn't recognize or knew only vaguely from other gatherings where I had failed to pay attention. The funeral was partly Buddhist to respect the wishes of Naoko's parents who flew in from Saitama, Japan. They had known about her cancer diagnosis and had visited a few times, but like us, were shocked at the sudden turn of events. Being a third-generation Japanese American from California, I was able to say a few words and phrases to them in Japanese. But through all the years I had known Naoko's parents, I had never felt warmth from either of them. They weren't huggers. They smiled and thanked me for taking care of her, even though it felt like the other way around, with her making most of the decisions in our family. Naoko had often said that she didn't want to end up like her parents in Japan, that she loved being a New Yorker, an international being who can transcend what was expected of her back home, which would have been to become a devoted stay-at-home wife and mother. She wouldn't have pursued a career in film. She loved being a creative professional in New York. She loved city life. She hated bugs, and would have hated it here in Dogwood where there's no Starbucks within 40 minutes and hardly any concrete sidewalks.

I can still hear that echo of their mourning, their sobs and gasps, their very real expressions of grief ("She was so young, how awful") against my own numb nothing. I remember spending most of that time holding Max's hand or patting his hair. He must have looked identical to me, with zero expression, hardly saying a word.

I continue watching and scrolling my phone, waiting for one of these fucking comedians to say something funny, but they never do.

I'm back in the same dream again. I'm in our old kitchenette in New York, waiting for the water to boil. The kettle is red like all the other appliances, a pattern that began with the red Dutch oven that Naoko's mother had bought us after we got married. There's a red stand mixer, red tea towels, red oven mitts, a stirring spoon with a red handle.

I'm there to make chamomile tea for Naoko. After the cancer

spread to her lungs, she got an oxygen nasal cannula to help her breathe, which meant she couldn't be near the gas stove due to the risk of explosion. The stove is on the highest flame setting, and I see Naoko walking slowly towards me, the oxygen tank on wheels behind her.

"*You shouldn't be here,*" I say. "*It's dangerous.*"

She laughs, which makes her cough.

"*What's so funny?*" I ask.

"*You,*" she starts, struggling with each word. "*Shouldn't. Be. Here. Either. Tom.*"

The doorbell is ringing, a series of loud, reverberating ding-dongs that instantly wakes me up. I feel Max squirming next to me. He pulls the duvet over his head, turning himself into a little lump. I get my glasses and check my phone to find more unread messages and the clock saying 9:54 a.m. It's been a while since we slept in like this.

A muffled voice from the lump says, "Is it the monster?"

I pat the top of what I think is his head. "The monster's not here. It's probably just a delivery or something."

When I finally get down and unlatch the front door, I see a woman in a red sports cap and a green Carhartt jacket. She's carrying a tin-foiled platter with one arm and uses the other to reach around my neck for a hug.

"Hey, Hoshie."

"Nora."

She and her husband Darrell gave me the nickname after my last name, Hoshino. We had worked together on the elk documentary a couple of years ago. I had stayed here in Dogwood for close to a month, and it quickly became a place I longed to come back to. Nora worked in the State Park Department and helped our crew with permits and other paperwork, while her husband Darrell, a park ranger—or "naturalist interpreter" as he called himself—stuck around with us during the entire shoot. He didn't need to, but we probably wouldn't have gotten our shots without him there.

It wasn't just that this natural landscape here was beautiful—it was them and their companionship that I could never forget. A friendship and bond I'd never had, even with some friends I'd known for years.

"I know it's impolite to show up unannounced, and I thought about calling you, but for the life of me I could not find your number! Anyway, Darrell said you were making the big move here and I had to see it for myself."

I had only let him know about the move while Max and I were waiting at the airline gate at LaGuardia for our flight to Tennessee. I remember making the decision to move here immediately after Naoko's funeral, but in the months leading up to it, I didn't have the heart to let anyone in Dogwood know until the very last minute, maybe because there was a small part of me that didn't think it would actually happen.

I lead Nora inside and she sets the covered platter on the kitchen counter. She asks when we got in.

"Just about three days ago."

"I wish you would have called us to help! There must have been a lot to move here.

"We sold a lot of things in New York, so…"

"Oh, honey," she says softly. "I'm so sorry. I was devastated when I saw the news. The tribute that one of her friends wrote on Facebook." She puts both her hands on her heart. "Just wow. I had no idea about all her accomplishments and those movies she made. She was so beautiful, too. How have you been holding up? How's the little one taking it? I just can't imagine…"

I smile in a way that I'm used to at this point, that's crafted to reassure the other person that I'm grieving but functional. "We're doing okay. I think leaving New York is also what we needed. Here, we can start fresh."

"Well, you take all the time you need, honey."

I wish she didn't call me that. When Naoko was alive, she never used cute nicknames. She had been cool, bordering on cold, and if she'd ever said "honey" it had been sarcastic.

"Daddy?"

I follow the voice behind me to find Max hugging the edge of the staircase. His hair is sticking up in every direction and he looks younger than he is, especially in those fleece pjs with spaceships printed on them.

"Aww, hello little sleepyhead." Nora crouches down and gestures for a big hug. "It's wonderful to finally meet you, sweet pea! Your daddy's told me so much about you."

Max remains frozen where he is. I mouth 'sorry' to Nora on his behalf.

"Oh that's alright," she laughs. "I don't blame him! Stranger danger! Not for long, though, I hope. I better get going anyhow. Darrell said he might drop by later with some beers, but I told him he should give you some time to get settled in first."

"That sounds great. I've really missed him. And you."

"Oh Hoshie, we missed you too, honey. So happy you're here."

We hug goodbye and Nora waves emphatically to Max, who's still unwilling to come down.

"Hey bud." I uncover the tin foil on the dish she left them. "Want some...mac and cheese for breakfast?"

After we finish getting ready, we head to the town—about 20 minutes away by car—and make the first stop at a little coffee shop called The Spotted Cow. It's run by a middle-aged couple and the walls are decorated with garish paintings (by Hank, the husband) of various spotted cows. We catch up, recognizing each other from the shoot, and I introduce them to Max, who's hiding behind my legs. They treat him to a giant chocolate chip cookie, and I get a dark roast coffee to go.

Outside, the air is crisp. Breathing feels nourishing, which is something I never felt in New York. The "town" is just a couple blocks long, but there are people out and about today, and every once in a while, someone looks at us and nods their head or says "Hi," with an added layer of affection towards Max. He has crumbs on his face from devouring the cookie, and I wipe it off with my palm.

"Stop," he winces. "I'm not a baby."

I ruffle his hair and he looks away, sullen. On the corner, there's a small farmer's market going on, and there's a boy, maybe a few years older than Max, managing one of the booths. The boy doesn't look particularly excited or happy, but he has polite manners and tells us all about the sandwich options for today: roast beef, pulled pork, turkey. He's wearing a red flannel shirt and cargo pants. Maybe Max can hang out with this kid. They can go fishing and hunting. Chop wood. But I look down at Max, and he's kicking some rocks with his shoes. He's lanky and uncoordinated in comparison to this sandwich stand kid. I get us a couple pulled pork sandwiches for the road.

Next we go inside the home goods store that also sells rainboots, Bibles, and alcohol.

"Hey there," the store clerk says. "Can I help you find something? You visiting?"

A few other customers turn their heads to look at us.

"We actually just moved here," I say.

"Oh yeah? Where from?"

"New York."

"Uh huh. You do look kind of familiar, though. Did you ever spend time around here with that park ranger?"

I explain that my crew and I did indeed spend time here to

watch elks, and yes, Darrell helped us through it all. "He made Dogwood seem like the perfect place to live."

"It sure is, isn't it."

The store clerk helps us locate some generic blue curtains and a packet of night lights. Max chooses a bag of peanut brittle and the store clerk asks if he's lost any teeth yet. Max shakes his head.

"These might help along with that," he says.

All of my friends in New York had begged me not to move here. They recommended grief therapy. A long vacation. *"You'd be the only Asians for miles,"* someone said during the haphazardly put-together goodbye party. This didn't bother me, knowing we'd actually be the only *people* for miles. *"What about Max? Is it really a safe place for him to grow up? With all that hate?"*

I reassured my friends that the South wasn't as scary as the news made it seem. *"I know these people. In some ways we'd be safer there than in New York."*

Some friends said I was going too far just to prove a point, that I had the habit of being a Devil's Advocate. Maybe there was some truth to that. Having traveled to different cities in the last decade, I was constantly surprised by Americans who lived in these kinds of rural areas. A lot of them had never interacted with Asians before, but I never felt that they were racist towards me. If we had opportunities for long conversations, which happened a lot while waiting for animals to appear in the wild, we would trade stories about our families, our grandparents, our food traditions. I would sometimes find myself telling them about my grandfather's incarceration at Manzanar during the war, stories that were difficult for me to hear growing up, and had been difficult for me to recount for most of my adulthood. Yet somehow, in places like these, the kindness of the people pulled these stories out of me, and I would listen to their stories in return.

Every time one of my New Yorker friends made some generalization about Midwesterners or Southerners, I would come to their defense and say: It's different from what you see on the news.

"You were only there for a limited amount of time," they'd counter. *"Maybe that's why they were so nice to you. You're talking about a permanent move. I get that you need something different, but this is too extreme."*

We drive another 20 minutes so that we can spend the rest of the afternoon at the state park where my crew, Darrell, and I spent twenty-six days following and watching elks. I'm hoping we'll come across one today, and that maybe Max will cheer up a little as a result.

As soon as we get out of the car, we're surrounded by trees with leaves of varying hues, in crimson, golden brown, and a deep dark purple. This foliage is one of the many things that blew me away the first time I came here.

I can see Max taking it all in, and for the first time since we made the big move, he looks at ease with where he's at. He's not clinging to me or trying to hide from anyone. Here, right now, it's just the two of us against all these trees, the giant sky, the pebbly roads sprinkled with pinecones.

"Is this where you shot the elks?" he asks.

"Filmed them. Yeah."

We both take a minute to look at everything before tacitly agreeing to start walking towards one of the trails. We stop every once in a while to notice moss, bugs, birds, centipedes, the different textures of bark. This right here is exactly what I had envisioned our new life to be, the two of us together, intrepid, observing nature and taking in its chaos and beauty.

Without Darrell, and with no signal on the GPS on my phone, it's hard to tell which path we need to take to have the best chance of coming across elks. I used to know this place so well.

"Rocks keep getting in my shoes," Max says. We check, and there are multiple holes now in his sneakers. I make a mental note to order him proper hiking shoes after we get home.

We keep walking, but in the end, we don't come across any elks, and we decide to head back to the car before the sun sets. Once we're back in the car, we eat our cold pulled pork sandwiches in silence and share a water bottle that's been there since a few days ago.

We stop at a grocery store called Porky and Chick's for milk, eggs, and the "right kind of peanut butter" (Creamy) to replace the "wrong kind" (Crunchy) that I bought on our first grocery run. At home, we reheat Nora's mac and cheese for dinner and settle into my bed, which we use like a couch. I have my laptop out at our feet so that we can watch PBS cartoons. We still don't have a TV.

"Daddy?"

"Yeah?"

"Will Mommy know to find us here?"

"What do you mean?"

"You know. When she visits."

I press pause on the video. I want to be careful about my response. For the most part, I consider myself a rational person, but conversations with Max were becoming more challenging than some of the philosophy exams I took back in college. I was used to having heavy conversations with him about cancer and death, especially in the last few months. Naoko had been the one to initiate it back when it seemed like she might still beat this thing, and she had always been better at communicating with him. I remember her trick, which was essentially what my professors used to do: answer every question with a question.

"What do you think?"

Max snuggles in closer. "I think so, I think she can find us."

I kiss the top of his head. He's lost that baby smell, but I can still remember kissing him exactly here, when his scalp was still soft.

"Daddy?"

"Yeah?"

"When are we going home?"

I press play on the cartoon. It's about a neurodivergent cat who's good at math.

"This is home," I say, our eyes fixated on the screen.

After Max falls asleep, I sneak out of the room and text Darrell to see if he's still up. It's a little past 9 p.m. and he texts back immediately to say he's on his way. While I wait, I wash the dishes and realize there's still so much we need to purchase for this kitchen to feel complete. We need a few more pots of different sizes and a proper kitchen towel to replace the bath towel hanging on the oven door. Spices. I forgot to take into account that we'd probably have to drive all the way to Nashville or Atlanta for the nearest Asian grocery store. Amazon probably delivers here. For the most part, we could fill the void with a series of Target runs, but still, the space feels so empty, not just because this house is bigger, but because our family has one less person in it.

Darrell texts to say he's here, being mindful not to wake up Max with the doorbell.

"My man!" he says, immediately coming in for a tight hug. "You're really here." He holds up a six-pack of IPAs, grinning with a child-like mischievousness. It's dark and cold outside, so I invite him inside to the kitchen, which is where our only chairs are.

"I can't believe you're really here." He shakes his head. "I thought you were one of those film people who would never come back. But here you are. That's a bold move, man. And hey, I know I said this over text and stuff, but I want you to know that I've been thinking of you and your family. You're literally in our prayers every night. What you've been through... I don't know what to say. I don't know what I'd do if Nora..." He lets his words trail off. For all his expertise on nature and the "circle of life," Darrell still can't say "death" or "cancer."

I say thanks and we each open a can.

"To Naoko," he says, the emphasis on the first syllable like he's saying "nay."

He looks around the room, at the boxes in the hallway, and says he knew the people who used to live in this house. "Big family. Something like five kids. They grew up and all moved away, and the empty nesters took their savings and moved down to Florida. Same old story, you know. People from out of town don't really decide to move here like you did, so I'm sure they were happy this house went to you guys." Darrell clears his throat. "Did I tell you we got a sixth one?"

"Another dog?"

"And here's the kicker. We named him Hoshie, after you! It's officially *Hoshino*, but Hoshie's easier to say when we're calling out for him."

I laugh in response and find myself looking down at the floor. The linoleum is clearly discolored in some places, something I hadn't noticed before. The ceiling light is too dim. I'll have to get a floor lamp.

"Hey man, you okay?"

"What? Oh right. Sorry." Darrell had just asked when the elk episode was going to air. "It already happened," I say. "Did I forget to send the link?"

"Don't worry about it. I should have just googled it anyway. I know you've been going through a lot." Darrell leans forward and says, "When people pass, they're not really gone, you know?"

I feel my heart sinking. Was it the fact that Darrell named

their new dog after me? What the fuck did it mean, anyway? Do they see me like a dog? A pet? Did they think it would make me feel better after what happened? Maybe I'm just tired and paranoid. But Naoko's words come back to me now, something she used to say every time I came back to New York from a place like Dogwood.

"Just because they're nice to you, doesn't mean they're better people. Anyone can be nice on the outside."

I can't deny the fact that I chose Dogwood, in part, to spite her. Like I could prove her wrong, after so many times in our marriage when she had the upper hand, the last laugh, the final word. Finally, I could do something she would have never said yes to. But let's say this experiment goes foul. I'm not going to sacrifice Max's happiness just to win an argument with my dead wife. It wouldn't be too late to turn back. We would lose more money on movers, and we would have to find a brand new rental in New York, which would likely mean settling for a place that's more expensive, possibly even smaller.

Outside, the wind is howling.

"Tell you what," Darrell says, putting his beer down. "I better get going. But we'll see more of each other real soon. What day is it today? Saturday? Okay, so come to our place next Friday night. Bring Max. We'll have a ton of people over. Nora always makes a shit ton of food and we'll have a good time. You can meet people, we can all help you out, alright? Some of them's got kids, I know at least one of them's got a boy around Max's age. Is he doing kindergarten or anything?"

"First grade."

"Time flies, my man. He was still really little the last time you were here."

I walk him out the door, and I look up to see thousands of stars. "I missed this," I say. "Out of all the places I've been, this was always my favorite."

Darrell laughs. "It's cool to hear a guy like you say that about our shit town—now it's your shit town too, I guess."

We say our goodbyes, I close the door, and drain the rest of my beer down the sink. I'm a little dizzy going up the stairs and slide into bed next to Max.

I'm back on the trail but this time, I'm by myself. The air is misty, and the trees are bare. There's a woman's voice off in the distance, like she's humming a song. I walk deeper into the trail, one foot after the other, trying to follow the voice. I approach a flat field and there it is, a magnificent elk. Judging by its enormous size and the shape of its antlers, it looks identical to the one we followed for the documentary. We nicknamed him Jack. He's looking off to the side, and I'm waiting for the perfect shot, when he'll turn to look my way. I'm now holding a camera even though it wasn't there before. Jack's ears twitch, indifferent to my presence, even as I walk closer towards him. I learned from the shoot that the elk can adapt and survive in a wide range of landscapes, from the lowland valleys to the Appalachians. They can sustain themselves on grass and their own stored fat. Some say it's the perfect mammal. As the elk turns, I make sure to capture him in all his glory, and as he turns more, the woman, who's still humming, reveals herself. She has long black hair, wearing a white frock, but her head is still hidden from the elk's antler and I can't see her face. I call out her name, and the elk, startled, gallops away.

I'm woken up by a clanking noise coming from one of the rooms downstairs. It sounds like pots and pans clanging, or an iron wind chime, though we don't own one. I look over at Max, still asleep, hogging most of the duvet like a giant cocoon. My phone says it's 2:26 a.m. The noise continues. I look around for my glasses and realize I'm still wearing them. I get out carefully so as not to wake Max and make my way downstairs. My body aches, probably from all the stuff I carried yesterday.

As the sound grows louder, I notice the culprit—the window above the kitchen is slightly open. It's been maybe four hours since Darrell was here. I must have opened it and forgotten about it. The wind from outside was making the ladles and spatulas clang from where they were hanging from their new hooks. I shut the window and go back upstairs.

On the way, I think I see something moving from the corner of my eye, something moving in Max's room. We had gotten curtains but I forgot about the rod. I move closer, and in the glimmer of the night light, I can see that the movement is just shadows from the tree branches outside. I should just go back to bed, but I find myself shuffling my feet deeper into Max's room. I sit cross-legged next to the window, watching the branches sway. The leaves are starting to fall. No monsters here. Just me and the trees, and an owl hooting in the distance.

I let my fingers graze the spines of the books on the shelf and stop at *Goodnight, Moon*. I hadn't listened to Naoko's voice at all, not even from videos on my phone or even the mundane voicemails she used to leave, either about how she's on her way home or asking when I was coming home.

I should just get it over with. Listen to her voice and move on.

I take a deep breath and press the button I hadn't pressed in a long time.

There's some static, and then a whisper. I close my eyes and it's like she's right there.

"Mom?"

Wait.

"Mom? Are you there?"

It's Max's voice. He must have recorded over it.

There's a clicking sound followed by more static. I flip through the pages of the book—the cow jumping over the moon, the kittens and mittens, the mush, hush. It's gone. Forever. Idiot. Max, but also me. I should have stored this book somewhere safer. I could have digitized the recording. I shouldn't have pressed it. Ignorance would have been bliss. I could have continued to believe that her voice was going to be accessible, without ever confirming it. It can't be that simple, could it? Is there another button on this book? Maybe it's hidden.

But then, there she is, in front of me. Long hair, not a wig, parted from the side. The white silk blouse she used to wear to work. Her focused, piercing gaze. "Hey you," she mouths, but only static comes out.

"Daddy? Wake up, Daddy."

CONTRIBUTORS

JOHN T. EDGE has written or edited more than a dozen books, served as culinary curator for the weekend edition of NPR's *All Things Considered*, and has been featured on dozens of television shows from *CBS Sunday Morning* to *Iron Chef*. He is a contributing editor at *Garden & Gun* and has served as a columnist for the *New York Times* and the *Oxford American*. He has won four James Beard Foundation awards including Beard's M.F.K. Fisher Distinguished Writing Award in 2012 and 2020. Edge holds an MA in Southern Studies from the University of Mississippi and an MFA in Creative Nonfiction from Goucher College. His 2017 book, *The Potlikker Papers: A Food History of the Modern South*, was named a best book of 2017 by NPR, *Publishers Weekly*, and a host of others. Since 2018, he has hosted the television show *TrueSouth*, which airs on the SEC Network and ESPN, and is available on Hulu. At the University of Mississippi, he directs the Mississippi Lab, serves as Writer-in-Residence in the Department of Writing and Rhetoric, and serves the Southern Foodways Alliance as the Founding Director. Edge is also developing the Greenfield Farm Writers Residency, set to open in the summer of 2025 at the University of Mississippi, which will pay stipends of $1,000 per week to writers in the overnight studios. Edge is a distinguished visiting professor in the MFA in Narrative Nonfiction program at the Grady College of the University of Georgia. Edge lives in Oxford, Mississippi, with his wife.

RANDI PINK, a native of Birmingham, Alabama, is a highly acclaimed author, educator, and jazz vocalist with a rich and diverse background. Graduating from the esteemed HBCU Alabama State University, she furthered her academic journey with a graduate degree from the University of Louisville, followed by the pursuit of a second graduate degree in Creative Writing from the University of Alabama at Birmingham. Renowned for her novels, including the critically acclaimed *Angel of Greenwood* and *Girls Like Us*, recognized as a School Library Journal Best Book of 2019, Randi's upcoming work, *Under the Heron's Light*, set in the historic Great Dismal Swamps, is poised for publication in October 2024.

CAMILLE BOXHILL is a Jamaican American writer currently based in South Florida. She earned an MA in Creative Writing with Distinction from the University of Bristol. Boxhill is an alumna of the 2022 Madeleine Milburn Mentorship Program and a 2022 Space to Write Project award recipient. She has also enjoyed support and recognition from Iowa Writers' Workshop Summer Program, Renaissance House, and Hurston/Wright Foundation. Her debut novel will explore themes of multigenerational trauma, legacy, and identity, alongside elements of Jamaican folklore. Boxhill is represented by the Madeleine Milburn Agency.

CONSTANCE COLLIER-MERCADO is an experimental writer, artist, and womanist culture worker committed to Black language and collective memory. Born in Chicago and raised in the Bronx, her political home resides in the space between family connections tied to Atlanta, GA; Bolivar County, MS; and Beaufort County/Gastonia, AfroCarolina. Consumed by ideas of global Blackness as polyamorous Church, she weaves this aesthetic into her practice via an irreverent blk gender-infinite.

ASHLEY BLOOMS (they/she) is the author of *Where I Can't Follow*, which was a finalist for the Weatherford Award. Their debut novel, *Every Bone a Prayer*, was long-listed for the Crook's Corner Book Prize. She's a graduate of the Clarion Writer's Workshop and received their MFA as a John and Renee Grisham Fellow from the University of Mississippi. Their fiction has appeared in *The Year's Best Dark Fantasy & Horror*, *Fantasy & Science Fiction*, and *Strange Horizons*, among others.

MAURICE CARLOS RUFFIN is the author of national bestseller *The American Daughters*, a New York Times Editor's Choice published by One World Random House. He is the recipient of the 2023 Louisiana Writer Award and the Black Rock Senegal Residency. He also wrote *The Ones Who Don't Say They Love You*, which was published by One World Random House in August 2021. His first book, *We Cast a Shadow*, was a finalist for the PEN/Faulkner Award, the Dayton Literary Peace Prize, and the PEN America Open Book Prize. Ruffin is the winner of several literary prizes, including the Iowa Review Award in fiction and the William Faulkner–William Wisdom Creative Writing Competition Award for Novel-in-Progress. A New Orleans native, Ruffin is a professor of Creative Writing at Louisiana State University.

MELISSA GINSBURG is the author of the novels *The House Uptown* and *Sunset City*, the poetry collections *Doll Apollo* (winner of the Mississippi Institute of Arts and Letters Poetry Award) and *Dear Weather Ghost*, and three poetry chapbooks, *Arbor*, *Double Blind*, and *Apollo*. Her poems have appeared in the *New Yorker*, *Image*, *Guernica*, *Kenyon Review*, *Fence*, *Southwest Review*, and other magazines. Originally from Houston, Texas, Melissa studied poetry at the Iowa Writers' Workshop. She is Associate Professor of Creative Writing and Literature at the University of Mississippi, and serves as Associate Editor of *Tupelo Quarterly*. She lives in Oxford, Mississippi.

JOANNA PEARSON is the author of the debut novel *Bright and Tender Dark*. Her second short story collection, *Now You Know it All*, was chosen by Edward P. Jones for the 2021 Drue Heinz Literature Prize and named a finalist for the Virginia Literary Awards. Her first short story collection, *Every Human Love*, was a finalist for the

Shirley Jackson Awards, the Janet Heidinger Kafka Prize for Fiction, and the Foreword INDIES Awards. Her fiction has appeared in *The Best American Short Stories, The Best American Mystery and Suspense, The Best Small Fictions, Best of the Net,* and many other places. Originally from western North Carolina, she now lives with her husband and two daughters near Chapel Hill, where she works as a psychiatrist.

F.E. CHOE is a Korean American writer whose work has been published in *Clarkesworld Magazine, The Moth Magazine,* and *Fractured Lit.* She is a 2023 graduate of the Clarion West Writers Workshop, a Viable Paradise alum, and an editor at *100 Word Story.* Born in Toronto, Canada, she currently lives in the United States.

YURINA YOSHIKAWA holds a BA from Barnard College and an MFA from Columbia University. Her writing has appeared in *The Atlantic, NPR, Lit Hub, The Japan Times, AAWW's The Margins, The New Inquiry, The Tennessean, The Pinch, Edible,* and elsewhere. She has been awarded the Tennessee True Stories Prize and fellowships from the Tennessee Arts Commission, Hewnoaks, Baldwin For The Arts, and the Southern Arts Prize's Tennessee State Fellowship. She has lived in Tokyo, Palo Alto, and New York before settling down in Nashville, where she lives with her husband and two sons. She is the Director of Education at The Porch Writers' Collective and hosts the Japanese literature book club for the Japan-America Society of Tennessee. For more information, visit yurinayoshikawa.com.

SPONSORS, DONORS, & PARTNERS

The Southern Prize and State Fellowships for Literary Arts is only possible through the generous community of support from individuals, foundations, and organizations.

JOHN T. EDGE

FRAN AND ARNOLD GELLMAN

ELLIOT KNIGHT

SEJAL MEHTA

TERRY AND SCOTT SHANKLIN-PETERSON

SUZETTE M. SURKAMER

ADDITIONAL DONORS AND SUPPORTERS

STATE ARTS AGENCIES

LITERARY ANTHOLOGY CREDITS

JOHN T. EDGE, Introduction
SUZETTE M. SURKAMER, Foreword

2024 SOUTHERN PRIZE AND STATE FELLOWSHIPS FOR LITERARY ARTS JURORS

BILL CHENG

GARRARD CONLEY

ABBY FREELAND

HARPER GLENN

RACQUEL HENRY

JASMINE MORRELL

JANAE NEWSOM

REYES RAMIREZ

MEG REID

JERID WOODS

SOUTH ARTS STAFF

MICHAEL BOSARGE, Vice President of Finance & Operations

TAYLOR DOOLEY BURDEN, Interim Director, Traditional Arts

HILLARY CRAWFORD, Assistant Vice President, Programs

JOSEPH CRAWFORD, Assistant Director, Programs

NIKKI ESTES, Director, Presenting & Touring

DAMIEN HARRISON, Accounting & Human Resources Manager & Accessibility Coordinator

CATHY LEE, Director, Database & Technology

CAROLINE MADDOX, Vice President of Advancement

DALYLA MCGEE, Development Officer

CHARLES PHANEUF, Vice President of Strategy

DMITRY PONOMARENKO, Accounting & Operations Manager

KARA QUEEN, Office and Administrative Services Manager

ERIC RUCKER, Assistant Director, Jazz

IVAN SCHUSTAK, Director, Communications

LISA E. SMALLS, Interim Director for Organization & Community Initiatives

EMMITT STEVENSON, Director, Artist Engagement

AIYANA STRAUGHN, Director, Arts Partnerships

SUZETTE M. SURKAMER, President & CEO

KARINA TEICHERT, Digital Content Manager

DREW TUCKER, Director, Jazz

MIRANDA VALERIO, Executive Assistant & Board Manager

SABRINA WILDER, Executive Team Administrative Manager

JORDAN YOUNG, Director, Media Arts & Design Manager

JOY YOUNG, Vice President of Programs

SOUTH ARTS BOARD OF DIRECTORS

HUB CITY PRESS STAFF

PUBLISHING
New & Extraordinary
VOICES FROM THE
AMERICAN SOUTH

FOUNDED IN Spartanburg, South Carolina in 1995, Hub City Press has emerged as the South's premier independent literary press. Hub City is interested in books with a strong sense of place and is committed to finding and spotlighting extraordinary new and unsung writers from the American South. Our curated list champions diverse authors and books that don't fit into the commercial or academic publishing landscape.

Funded by the National Endowment for the Arts, Hub City Press books have been widely praised and featured in *the New York Times*, the *Los Angeles Times*, *NPR*, *the San Francisco Chronicle*, *the Wall Street Journal*, *Entertainment Weekly*, *the Los Angeles Review of Books*, and many other outlets.

HUB CITY PRESS books are made possible through the generous support of grants and donations from corporations, state and federal grant programs, family foundations, and the many individuals who support our mission of building a more inclusive literary arts culture in the South, in particular: Byron Morris and Deborah McAbee, Charles and Katherine Frazier, and Michel and Eliot Stone. Hub City Press gratefully acknowledges support from the National Endowment for the Arts, the Amazon Literary Partnership, the South Carolina Arts Commission, the Chapman Cultural Center, Spartanburg County Public Library, and the City of Spartanburg.